MATILDA'S
BLOOMERS

To Tim
Best Wishes
from
Marjorie Northcutt

MATILDA'S BLOOMERS

PRAIRIE SCHOOL STORIES

MARJORIE NORTHCUTT
ILLUSTRATED BY BECKY BRYANT

Hearth
PUBLISHING
HILLSBORO, KANSAS

Matilda's Bloomers
© 1993 by Marjorie Northcutt

First Edition
Printed in the USA
by Multi Business Press, Hillsboro, Kansas

Illustrations: Becky Bryant

Publisher's Cataloging in Publication
(Prepared by Quality Books Inc.)

Northcutt, Marjorie
    Matilda's bloomers: prairie school stories / Marjorie
Northcutt.
    p. cm.
    Preassigned LCCN: 93-61048.
    ISBN 1-882420-09-8

    1. Middle West (U.S.)–Fiction. 2. Teaching–Fiction.
I. Title.

PS3564.O783M38 1993   813'.54
                             QBI93-21759

To all the children with whom I've shared a classroom.
Marjorie Northcutt

To my grandmothers—
Whose stories, just like Marjorie Northcutt's, have taken me to a different time and place in my illustrations for Matilda's Bloomers.

Becky Bryant

Special thanks to:
    Sue Williams
    Linda Hubalek
    and our families

TABLE OF CONTENTS

INTRODUCTION

What comes to mind when you see an old deserted schoolhouse out in the middle of nowhere? Maybe some of the glass panes are gone in the windows that march along the sides of the building. The belfry is absent its original song maker, but a variety of birds have taken up residence now that the clanging of the bell is gone. Because of the blowing wind, the weathered seesaw bumps the dirt, wearing a bare spot in the playground now reclaimed by the tall prairie grass. Weeds have regained their footing around the front steps.

Young people just barely glance at the old building with the peeling white paint as they speed by. But the older generation pauses, and with a flick of their memory, they can transform that same building into the schoolhouse of their youth.

The seesaw is going wild as an older boy on the one end thumps the ground with all his might. The three little girls on the high end squeal as their bottoms lift off the board for a second and come down hard as gravity takes hold.

One group of youngsters are playing a game of ante-over as they heave the ball over the carriage roof to the group waiting on the other side.

The schoolmarm, in her dark flowing skirt and long-sleeved white blouse, is standing on the bottom step of the building entrance, watching the children delight in a new day. She turns and gathers her skirt slightly with one hand to step back into the schoolhouse. It's time to ring the morning bell to start another day of school.

Reminisce back to those school days when you read the stories in *Matilda's Bloomers*.

Linda K. Hubalek
Hearth Publishing

CATCH THE KID-WAGON

The years have come and the years have gone, but I can still hear my mother calling, "Hurry, hurry, or you won't catch the kid-wagon." And every morning, it was the same hurry, scurry, dash around, look for this, look for that. Pinkie was the one who always held us up. He could never find two socks that matched, or more than one of his shoes. But somehow, miraculously, in all those years, we never missed getting to the corner on time. Out the door, down the driveway, out past the old cottonwood, and on to the corner, we always managed to be there when Jake Pettycore pulled up. He would yell a mighty, "Whoa!" bringing his team of sorrels to a snorting stop.

My friend, Faye, always saved a place for me. Pinkie sat close by, which was a good thing, as I could look him over to see if he had his shoes on the right feet, or if his overall straps were twisted. More than once, I remember taking his shirt off so I could turn it right-side-out, and help him put it back on again, while the little girls around us giggled and pretended to look the other way.

The big boys always sat in the back of the kid-wagon. Although Chauncy was one of the big boys, he sat in the middle, and I figured he sat there so he could tease the children on all sides of him. Usually it was the little ones he picked on, but he seemed to get a special pleasure out of heckling Lula, a big red-haired girl, who had a temper that was a good match for Chauncy's mean streak. Lula was an only child and had a store-bought lunch-pail. When Chauncy's teasing got too much, Lula would raise her lunch-pail and bring it down hard on Chauncy's head.

1

Chauncy warded off these attacks with a laugh. "You'll just break up your fancy lunch-pail," he warned.

"My Dad says he'll buy me as many lunch-pails as I can break up over your head," she would fume, so angry she seemed to be steaming, as her pinkish complexion turned to beet red.

Chauncy surprised us one morning as he called out, "'Button, Button?' I have a button this morning."

Chauncy never played games with us on the kid-wagon. "Maybe he's turned over a new leaf," I whispered to Faye.

Chauncy's eyes were deep blue with overhanging eyebrows. I'm almost ashamed to tell this, but when I looked at Chauncy, I thought of our old mule, Buck. Papa always said that Old Buck was the meanest critter on our farm, and Old Buck had deep-set eyes with over hanging brows just like Chauncy.

We placed our hands in front of us, palms together, waiting for Chauncy to start around. "Button, Button," he'd say, as he went down one side of the kid-wagon and up the other, his palms together, sliding his hands between our outstretched hands. Chauncy had named Faye to be "It", so she was the one to guess who had the button. Chauncy went all around one time savoring the suspense, as we all waited our turn, hoping that Chauncy would drop the button in our hands. Halfway around the second time, we all jumped nearly out of our skins as we heard the awfullest screaming you ever heard in all your life.

Chauncy had just passed Lula's freckled hands when it happened. We saw Lula jump up, shake her hands frantically, and run screaming to the back of the kid-wagon. She kept up the screaming as she jumped up onto a back bench and gathered her skirts around her knees. Chauncy was laughing as he picked up a little garter snake from the floor where Lula had dropped it. He held it up, dangling it over one finger. To Chauncy, it was the supreme joke.

To Jake the driver, it was a senseless piece of tomfoolery. He pulled up the reins, gave his loud "Whoa" message to the big sorrels. "Get rid of that!" he commanded in a stern voice.

With a sheepish grin, Chauncy stood up, leaned over, and

tossed the little reptile out into the weeds by the roadside. Calm settled over the kid-wagon. Lula stayed in the back of the vehicle, all the time glaring like an angry bull at Chauncy. He seemed unaware of her stare as he sat there with a smirky grin on his face.

After school, we always found our kid-wagon waiting in front of the school building, and we would climb aboard and be off for home. We were indifferent to the hardness of the benches and to the bumps and jolts as the kid-wagon bounced over the ruts on the two miles of hard-pan before we hit the sand.

A mile from school one evening we passed by a road crew. "There's your Papa," Faye exclaimed. "There in front of the wagon."

"I know," I told her. "I heard him tell Mama this morning that he had to get his poll tax worked off. Pinkie, " I said, turning to my little brother. "See Papa out here. Wave at him."

"See Papa out here," Chauncy mimicked in sugary tones. "See your Papa, Pinkie."

"You tend to your own business, Chauncy, or my Papa will come to your house and tell your father just how bad you are."

"I'm real scared," Chauncy taunted, but he did keep still.

Two miles from school the kid-wagon passed an apple orchard. Jake always slowed his horses down to a creepy walk while most of us jumped out of the kid-wagon, crawled through the fence, and picked up two or three red apples from the ground where the wind had blown them down. Then we would run to catch the wagon and climb back on. I always got one for Pinkie, as his legs were too short to make the run and catch the kid-wagon again. After we were all back on the wagon, Jake would whip up the horses to a good trot to make up the lost time, chewing on an apple as he drove, for someone always brought him one.

Chauncy was always the last one back on the kid-wagon, for he usually searched for the very best apples, and instead of picking up two or three, he filled his pockets and picked them off the trees.

This time Jake was muttering as Chauncy sauntered

4

back to the wagon. "Ought to run off and leave him," he groused.

That evening when Papa came in from his work on the roads, he noticed the half-eaten apple Pinkie had left on the table. "Where'd the apple come from? he asked.

"It's Pinkie's, Papa. We got it in Mr. Crockett's orchard."

"In Mr. Crockett's orchard? Did you pay for it?"

"No, Papa. All the kids get apples. Mr. Crockett told Jake to let us have them. He said he didn't want the ones on the ground."

"I don't like you getting apples and not paying for them," Papa insisted, "but if you're sure he doesn't use the ones on the ground, I suppose it's all right."

"Chauncy picks them off the trees," I volunteered.

"Chauncy has some hard lessons to learn," Papa told me.

The next morning on the kid-wagon, Chauncy seemed to be at his worst, taunting and teasing. Suddenly Jake's voice rang out. "Whoa!" and the sorrels stopped. We all looked at Jake. He turned around and looked at Chauncy. After staring at him for a minute, he said, "Chauncy, I've asked you to stop teasing children on this wagon. I even spoke with your father. It hasn't stopped you. Now you may find yourself on the bottom end of a joke soon, and if that doesn't stop you, you're going to have to walk to school or get your own ride."

Chauncy ducked his head and was quiet the rest of the way to school.

We all hoped Jake had settled him down, but on the ride home, Chauncy seemed to have forgotten Jake's waring. He teased everyone, especially Lula. Finally he started chanting:

"Lula, Lula, looks like an elephant,
Looks like an elephant, walks like a goose.
She has ears as long as a donkey,
And she has a face like a mountain moose."

I was glad when we came to the apple orchard. As we grabbed apples, I tried to console Lula. "Don't even listen to him, Lula, but if you do decide to bang him over the head with

your lunch-pail and it breaks, you can use mine. We have a new syrup bucket at home I can use."

"Thanks, but I think Jake's about ready to put him off the kid-wagon," Lula commented hopefully.

As usual, we all got back into the kid-wagon and settled into our seats, with Chauncy still picking apples. As he started to crawl through the fence, Jake yelled to us, "Hang on, kids. We're going for a ride."

He yelled "Giddy-up" and slapped the reins on the backs of the sorrels. The kid-wagon lurched forward. We held on as the wagon rattled over holes and bumps. It was a rough ride. We looked back and Chauncy was running to catch us. Everybody laughed and shouted. Down the road behind us, Chauncy kept running and shouting and waving his arms. Then someone started singing:

> "Chauncy, Chauncy, looks like an elephant,
> Looks like an elephant, walks like a goose.
> He has ears as long as a donkey,
> He has a face like a mountain moose."

Finally, we lost sight of Chauncy. I felt a little pang of sadness to realize that no one really cared.

Jake knew that he might lose his job for running off and leaving Chauncy, so he finally decided to stop and wait for him. We got off at our corner and started home. Just as we passed the cottowood on the way home, we saw the kid-wagon still waiting and Chauncy just coming over the hill east. We figured Jake would take him the last mile home.

We warned Pinkie to keep still about it at home, as we decided not to mention it to Mama or Papa. Some things are better left to die.

The next morning, Chauncy was a changed boy. He sat meekly in his corner and said nothing. A few days later, Chauncy did start talking to us, but never again did he tease anyone.

Once again, there was peace in the kid-wagon, and once again, we played "Button, Button", "Pussy Wants a Corner", and other games to pass the time.

And at home, every morning, there was Mama's voice calling to us, "Hurry, hurry, or you won't catch the kid-wagon."

SASSY SIDNEY

It was my first day of teaching, and I could only wonder how it would be. There, in a little one-room country schoolhouse with fifteen students, grades one through eight, I started out. I felt comfortably sure I knew a lot about school, after just finishing twelve years of it. To be eligible to teach, I had passed a state examination covering the basic subjects. Now here I was, anxious and eager to start the business I would be in the rest of my life.

Children in those days were supposed to be seen and not heard. They were sent to school with this admonition, "You get into trouble at school and you are in trouble at home." Children treated all authority with respect, and discipline problems were rare.

Sidney did not fit that pattern. He was the lone sixth grader at Valley School that year. He was a little thin wiry fellow, but I soon found out that what he lacked in height and weight, he made up for in spunk and spirit. When I looked at Sidney, I was a little disturbed to notice that his pale blue eyes seemed cold and calculating for one so young.

That first day at school, there had been showers throughout the morning. After the noon recess, the children came to the door, shuffling and scraping to get the mud and sand off their shoes.

I stopped Sidney at the door. "You forgot to scrape your shoes," I told him.

"Is that an order," he challenged. "This isn't the army, you know."

I was relieved to see him make a pretense of going back and scraping mud.

On Saturday, I met Sidney's mother in the little grocery store. She was a tall dignified-looking lady in a long black skirt and a white lace-collared blouse. I complimented her on Sidney's math ability and she replied, "He has four brothers and sisters to coach him, and four to tease and aggravate him. Don't take any sass off him," she warned. "His father and I don't at home." I noticed she had the same pale blue eyes as Sidney, but oh, so different. Kindly, tired-looking eyes, they were.

By the end of September, we had settled into a good routine. The county superintendent visited one day, and I must admit I was a little scared to have her observe my teaching. I breathed an audible sigh of relief when she turned and waved at me, and I saw the door close behind her.

Sidney waved his hand and I nodded to him. "My Uncle Edward teaches school, Miss Lillie," he began. "The county superintendent visited him last week, and he said he got a good rating. How do you think you rated, Miss Lillie?"

"If you were working when she stopped at your desk, I probably rated all right, Sidney."

I was glad to see Sidney liked to read when he finished his lessons, for when he was not busy, he was thinking up some type of strategy for heckling me. There were very few extra books for free reading in the room. I had brought some from home which my brothers and sisters had read, and the children had loaned some to the school. My father was angry when I spent a month's salary of fifty-five dollars as down payment on a set of books called *Book of Knowledge*. The children enjoyed browsing through those books.

Usually, to save time, I ran off the week's assignments on a hektagraph, but on the first Monday in October, I had failed to get it done, and was writing them on the board. I finished them just as the children came in and settled into their seats. In the quiet of the morning, Sidney's voice rang out loud and clear.

"Miss Lillie," he called out. "Miss Lillie, you misspelled tyranny. It has two 'n's."

How could I? I looked at the blackboard. Sure enough, I had left out one of the "n's". I felt my face blushing bright red,

as Sidney beamed in triumph. I knew how to spell tyranny. Why had I written the assignment so fast as to have misspelled a word? I tried to make a brave recovery.

"I surely did, Sidney," I admitted. "Why don't you correct it for me, while I check the roll. And thanks, Sidney, for catching it." Sidney was supremely happy. But he wasn't finished. He changed the spelling, laid the chalk down, and said in mock seriousness, "Miss Lillie, you'd better stay after school and write this word a few hundred times." When I heard a few smothered giggles around the room, I felt a firm conviction that I had to find some solution to this situation. I felt as if I were being dragged into a quagmire by this little fifty pound scrap of humanity.

On the following Friday, we worked right through our recesses and saved an hour for a baseball game. We had been using a board for a bat, a rubber ball for a baseball, and trees for bases. Now Mrs. Coombs, who had a son in seventh grade, had given us a new bat, a real baseball, two gloves and a mitt. She had made bases out of some old overalls. So excitement ran high as we headed for the playground.

I joined the fun to make eight on each side. We didn't call balls, and the first and second graders got to hit until they got a strike. Everyone took turns pitching, and the game was nearly over when I came up to bat the last time. I saw that it was Sidney pitching. I thought of fanning out to make him feel good, but then I told myself, "I probably will anyway, so I'd better just try."

It seemed to me that Sidney had a malicious grin on his face as he wound up to pitch. The first pitch was a low ball. The next one was inside, but I decided to swing at it. The bat hit the ball at an odd angle, causing it to glance off the bat, hit me in the mouth and fall at my feet. I dropped the bat and started to spit out bits of chipped teeth and then blood from a cut lip. All the children gathered around me, murmuring little words of sympathy.

I hadn't known Sidney's brother John was there watching the end of the game until I heard him lash out at him. "Sid, why did you do that?" he shouted. "You can throw a ball better than that."

"No, John, it was just an accident," I told him.

John came over and looked at my mouth. "I'll have my mother call Mrs. Coombs. She'll take you to the dentist over at Colcord."

I mumbled a "Thanks" through a swollen lip. "Tell the children to go on home, John." Inside the schoolhouse, I gathered up my homework and started to lock up, thinking I would wait on the steps for Mrs. Coombs. I was ready to step outside when I saw Sidney, sitting at his desk, shoulders slumped and head down.

"This can't be Sidney," I thought. I went over and stood by his desk for a few seconds, waiting silently. He did not look up as he toyed with a piece of paper on his desk.

"Sidney," I began, "it was not your fault. The bat hit the ball and it bounced over into my face. You didn't make it happen."

Sidney still did not look at me. I saw his lip quiver. The cocky Sidney of yesterday was gone. His voice came out soft and meek. "I tried to fan you," he said. "I threw it in too close."

"It's all right, Sidney. The dentist can smooth my teeth off, and I'll be fine," I assured him. "Come on Sidney, let's go home. And don't let your brother John tell you it was your fault. It wasn't."

Sidney took a deep breath and got out of his seat. He looked up at me. "Sorry it happened," he said. Then his face spread into a grin. "You do look funny, Miss Lillie." I put my arm around his shoulder and we walked to the door. I felt that we were friends now, and that we would be friends for always.

NATHAN, REFORM SCHOOL BOY

They called it "Frog Holler", "Frog Holler School". The little one-room frame building had two tall narrow outhouses by the back fence, and along the fence was a row of tall cottonwoods. A spindly elm grew by the school pump, one the children and I had set out in the fall.

That evening in February, the students, ranging from first grade to eighth, had called "Good-bye" as they left for home. I turned to erase the blackboard when a noise at the door made me turn to see which child had forgotten something. There, standing in the door was Nathan, the new boy. He was seventeen and stout built for his age. I was eighteen.

"I'd be scared of that kid, Miss Lillie. He's been in reform school."

Jim Brown's words echoed in my ears as I stood there. My heart leapt into my throat, and I stood as if frozen. I can still see him plain as day, as he stood there framed by the hall doorway. He was stocky, with short-cropped brown hair and narrow eyes as black as chinaberry beads. I noticed he was trying to smile, but it looked strangely sinister, not friendly. In a flash, I saw my predicament. If I'd only followed the children to the door to wave good-bye, then I could have watched him leave with the others. But now it was too late.

"Miss Lillie." Fear consumed me, and I stood as if paralyzed. My mouth was dry as cotton and I could not utter a sound.

His voice floated around the room, "Miss Lillie—Miss Lillie—Miss Lillie."

I was conscious that he was trying to tell me something.

"Miss Lillie, I'm supposed to do something—some work—for nothing, I mean. No pay. Work for somebody. 'Course I work at my sister's for my keep, but that doesn't count. Has to be for someone outside the family. If I could sweep out for you every night and lock up, you could go on home. I promise to do it good. I have to report back next Saturday, and if I could say I's doin' this, it would help."

"Report back?" I asked lamely, still so frightened I could hardly stand. I had started trembling all over and I hoped he didn't notice.

"My sister said I should ask you." He hesitated, waiting for me to respond. "If you don't want me, it's all right." He dropped his eyes and turned to go.

I found my voice, although it sounded weak and shaky coming out of my mouth. "Why Nathan, I think that's fine, a really good idea. I'll just gather up my things and get started home."

Maybe it was the late sun shining in through the west windows, but Nathan's face suddenly lighted up, transforming it into a friendly glowing countenance.

I picked up only half of what I needed and scooted hurriedly past him, as he looked for the broom in the cloak room. "What have I done?" I thought. "What if he takes things? But what's in this little old schoolhouse anyone would want? What will the school board say? Maybe fire me." Then I knew I didn't care what the school board would say. I just knew I had to get out of there.

By the time I had walked the mile and a half to the Shelby house where I was boarding, my heart had stopped pounding. The shakiness was gone, but my mouth was still dry and cottony. I was beginning to hear the sounds around me as I walked along, a frog's rhythmic croaking in the pond across the fence, a dick-sissel singing from a telephone pole, the distant barking of a dog. I had stopped hearing the husky voice of Nathan's "Miss Lillie—Miss Lillie—Miss Lillie."

The next morning at seven-thirty, I unlocked the door with the skeleton key and hesitated, feeling a bit uneasy at entering. I chided myself and stepped over the doorsill. There it was, everything in place with the floor swept, the board cleaned, and the broken window shade mended. I picked up an eraser and found it cleaned better than usual.

By eight o'clock, I could hear the children gathering on the playground. At nine, Callie rang the bell to bring them in, and they were soon settled into the double desk seats. Nathan was the last one to come in, and all the way to his seat, he looked at me with a questioning look on his face.

"Children," I announced, "Nathan is cleaning the room for us now. You did a good job, Nathan. Let's all say thanks to him." A unison of thanks brought a smile to his face.

I marvelled at the new Nathan that day. His chin was a little higher, and a camaraderie was developing with the other

boys. Lonnie came in at one o'clock, bragging about a winning ball game.

"Yes, but you had Nathan," the other boys countered.

By Friday, I felt at ease finishing up my work as Nathan cleaned the room. Sensing that I needed quiet, he always worked steadily and quietly.

Friday evening, as I gathered up my sack of papers and started to leave, Nathan came in with the erasers he had cleaned.

"Miss Lillie, could you write a paper sayin' I been workin'?" he asked. "We're goin' to Helena tomorrow, and they might not believe me if I didn't have a paper."

"Why sure, Nathan, I'll be glad to." I wrote the note verifying that he had cleaned the room and that he had done a good job.

"Thank you, thank you," he said appreciatively. He followed me to the door and stood on the step.

"How are you going to Helena?" I asked him.

"My sister. My sister and Jack. Jack's her husband. We're gonna try to get Joey."

"Who's Joey?"

"He's a little kid. He's only seven. The kids tease him. Sometimes he cries."

"What's a seven-year-old doing at reform school?"

"I heard them say there was no room at the orphan's home. My sister wants him. She says we'll fatten him up. He's a skinny little kid."

I started to go, then I turned back. "Nathan?"

He stopped at the door.

"Why were you in a reform school?"

There was no hesitancy, no reluctance in his answer. "It was my grandfather, Miss Lillie. He always whipped us kids. He was mad because my dad ran away and my mother died and he had to keep us. He would whip us for no reason at all, especially if he got too much home brew down him. My sister ran away and got married. Then he seemed to beat me more. I guess I just got tired of it that day. I threw up my arm to grab the strap, and Grandpa lost his balance and fell. He hit his head on an old anvil and it knocked him out. They said I attacked him. But I didn't, Miss Lillie, I didn't." His eyes pleaded for my acceptance of his story.

I saw honesty in his countenance. "I believe you, Nathan. I believe you." Relief showed in his face. After a moment of silence, I turned to go. "Don't forget to lock up," I said, more as a parting salute than as an admonition. Somehow, I had come to believe that Nathan would do things right.

THOMAS TILLOTSON
AND THE BIG SNOW

"**M**iss Lillie, Miss Lillie, we got a new kid and he's a boy." Rusty Robson shouted the news as he bounded into the schoolroom through the open schoohouse door. I put the chalk on the blackboard tray and turned to welcome the new boy. At the door stood a slender well-groomed woman. I was struck by a look of sadness on her face, and her thin cautious smile seemed to lose itself in that sadness.

"I want to enroll my son, Thomas, in beginning school," she said. Her voice had a soft English accent.

"He hasn't been in school before?" I asked.

"Only two weeks, where we lived in Huntington, England, but I can help him catch up," she promised.

"I'm sure we can both help him," I told her. "Bring him to school and we'll see."

"I brought him. Here's Thomas," the woman said and pulled a small boy from behind her skirts. I remembered later that all I saw of him was the big dark eyes and the sadness of his mother reflected in his face. There was a look of shyness, too, even a look bordering on fear in the little boy who clung so close to his mother.

Although the bell had not rung, the children had all taken their seats and sat staring at the new little boy. And, to them, he could not have looked more different if he had come from another planet. Here was a little boy in blue serge shorts, a white starched shirt, knee stockings, and black patent leather shoes. While his mother filled out the

enrollment form, he continued to stay close beside her.

From the enrollment form, I could see that the father was deceased, and that the mother was Elizabeth Tillotson. "Mrs. Tillotson," I said, "here's an empty seat that looks about right for Thomas. Here, let's try it out, Thomas." I took the hand nearest me, and Rusty tried to take the other. But Thomas would not budge. When his mother moved toward the seat, he moved with her. No amount of coaxing could loosen his firm grip on her skirt. I gave up, but Rusty stuck with him. Mrs. Tillotson glanced alternately at me in embarrassment and at Thomas in exasperation.

"Mrs. Tillotson, why don't you and Thomas visit for a while. Sit back here. Rusty, please get one of the small chairs for Thomas. Now, Mrs. Tillotson, stay as long as you like. Maybe if you visit every day for a while, Thomas might change his mind about school."

Thomas did not use the little chair—he stood close to his mother and stared at us with his big brown eyes. At ten o'clock, Mrs. Tillotson waved her hand at me and they walked out.

On the third morning, he sat on the chair, and on the fifth morning I suggested that she leave him there and go home. While he was engrossed in watching the third graders feeding a frog they had found at the creek, she slipped out, closing the cloak room door quietly behind her. Almost immediately, Thomas was aware that his mother was gone. I saw the look of fright on his face, and wondered what he would do. Before I could move to reassure him, he got up and went to the door, where he stood staring down at the floor. I started to go to him but Rusty was there first. Rusty took his hand, and the two stood there, Rusty looking at Thomas, and Thomas looking down at the floor. When I saw a big tear roll out of one of those big brown eyes and trace a path down his cheek, I decided to see how far Mrs. Tillotson had gone.

When I opened the door to the cloak room, I bumped into her. She stood there waiting and listening. She started to stammer out an apology, but I stopped her.

"Mrs. Tillotson," I said, "take Thomas home. Wait until he

gets over being frightened of school. Give him time—time to adjust to a new country and new people."

Mrs. Tillotson sighed a sigh of great relief. She took Thomas by the hand and walked away.

In the weeks that followed, I visited Mrs. Tillotson a few times. Usually Thomas was in the yard playing with a little wagon, or in a swing that hung in a big elm tree. I always waved at him. At first, he made no response, but finally one day, he waved back. I learned that they had come to live on the old Tillotson place when Tom Tillotson had been killed in a marketplace when a deranged man had gone berserk and killed three people. Thomas had been with his father at the time. Elizabeth Tillotson and Thomas had come to our rural Midwest community when Tom's parents had asked them to bring Tom's body back to the United States for burial.

I suggested to Mrs. Tillotson that she ask Rusty Robson over to play on Saturdays. I also suggested that she buy him some overalls and heavy shoes, so he would look like the other boys at school.

One Monday morning, Rusty burst into the schoolroom with great news. Thomas Tillotson had come to his house on Saturday. "We runned all over the pasture to catch a cottontail, but we never could catch him. And we rode old Gypsy up and down the cow-path, up and down, up and down."

Mrs. Tillotson had borrowed some books from school, and Thomas seemed to be keeping up. One day, Mrs. Tillotson appeared at the schoolhouse door. Thomas was with her, and I was glad to see a new look on his face, still shy, but no longer sad or frightened.

"Miss Lillie," she said, "Rusty's mother says the parents take turns bringing hot meals to school at noon. I'd like to bring one some day."

"Next Friday is not taken yet, Mrs. Tillotson. It would be great if you could bring it that day."

All day Thursday and Thursday night, snow had fallen. I stayed with the Collins family, a mile from school, and in bad weather Mrs. Collins took us to school in the Model T. I was wondering if we could get through the big drifts when Chris Collins spoke up. "I'll take you and the children to school in the wagon. The Ford would never make it."

Susan Collins looked out the kitchen window. "The drifts have covered the fenceposts," she observed.

On the way to school, the drifts were really high, but the big bays pulled us through. Puff clouds of steam blew from their nostrils as they plowed along. The world was covered with a beautiful glistening white, with even the tree branches hanging full.

There were still live coals in the stove where we had banked it the night before. Chris Collins threw in another bucket of coal, and the stove was soon warming up the room.

Excitement always ran high with the first big snow. Children came in to leave books, then ran right back out to play in the snow. Some of them stopped long enough to fire questions at me. "Can we play Fox and Geese, Miss Lillie? Can we have a snowball fight?"

Mrs. Tillotson came in with Thomas close beside her. Rusty Robson had his hand. Clyde Robson carried in a big pot of stew and put it on the stove.

"Mrs. Robson lent me her big stew pot," Mrs. Tillotson explained. "I hope the children like the stew. Mrs. Robson told me to put beef and vegetables in it. Mr. Robson picked us up and brought us to school with his big team of horses and wagon."

"They'll like the stew," I promised. "By noon, they are hungry enough to eat a horse."

Rusty Robson let out a whoop. "Hungry enough to eat a horse!" he shouted.

I could see that it was going to take a while to get the children settled down, so I asked Rusty to ring the bell to bring the snow revelers in from outside.

I turned to Mrs. Tillotson. "Why don't you stay and visit school today, Mrs. Tillotson? Clyde Robson will have to pick up the children at four. It will be one more chance for Thomas."

"Oh, —all right. I'll stay."

My hopes for Thomas were dashed when I saw him break away from Rusty and move back to his mother's chair.

As I started the day, I could see that it was going to be hard for the children to settle down into their usual good study pattern. "Boys and girls, work hard on your daily assignments, and if you finish everything, see if you can memorize eight or ten lines of Whittier's *Snowbound*. You'll find copies of the poem on the reading table. Then we'll skip morning recess and use all our time at noon for snow games." Everyone seemed happy at the suggestion and the room was full of quiet workers.

I called the first grade reading class and Rusty and his two classmates came up to the reading bench. I handed an extra book to Rusty. "Take this book back to Thomas," I suggested. "He can hear us read."

Thomas' face lighted up as he saw the book. He forgot his shyness as he said softly, "I have this book at home. I can read it."

Rusty took him by the hand, pulled a little, and Thomas came unglued from his chair. It was hard to believe my eyes when I saw him stand up and walk with Rusty to the reading bench. He sat down beside Rusty and waited.

"I think it would be fun to start a little differently this morning," I told them. "Before we read, let's tell something we saw on the way to school this morning, something different, something you didn't see yesterday."

The little girls were excited about a world that was all white, "Everything shines like diamonds," one said. "I saw a rabbit hopping," another told us.

Then it was Rusty's turn. "Well, Miss Lillie," he began, "I want to tell you something. The snow was so deep, those old horses was just draggin' their bellies on the snow. Yes, Ma'am, just draggin' their bellies."

I glanced at Mrs. Tillotson. She was hiding a smile behind her hand.

"And Thomas," I encouraged. "What did you see?"

I expected no response. But Thomas opened his mouth and the words came out, words couched slowly and carefully.

28

"Well, Miss Lillie, It's just like Rusty said. Those old horses was just draggin' their bellies on the snow..."

This time, I saw Mrs. Tillotson's eyebrows arched a bit quizzically, but her face was beaming.

I decided that it was a most beautiful day. Outside, everything was covered in dazzling white; inside everything was bathed in peace and happiness, with the aroma of vegetable stew scenting the schoolroom air. And Thomas was out of his shell, unafraid and comfortable in our midst.

Silently I thought to myself, "Bless you, Rusty Robson. Bless you and your fat-bellied horses."

A BROKEN HEART

He had just turned seven, and with golden curls, sky-blue eyes, and an impish grin, he could have passed for the genuine storybook pixie. "I should move him to the back of the room, " I told myself, "then he would not have to turn around backwards all the time to look at Lucretia." He wasn't bothering anyone, unless it bothered Lucretia for him to sit there staring at her with that little grin on his face. Lucretia was indeed a little beauty with her olive skin, dreamy dark eyes, and black hair pulled back in two braids.

I left my reading class, walked to Cory's desk and gently turned him around. I pointed to the math paper, and he started working on the lesson. I sat down with the reading class and glanced back across the room. There was Cory, turned around backwards again.

A few minutes later, Annette, the little busybody of the room, was at my side whispering. "Cory's crying," she informed me. I looked at Cory. His head was down on his desk. I was too busy with the reading class to give him my attention.

When the bell rang for recess, the children hurried past me. I had forgotten Cory, until I saw him at the end of the line, shuffling along, sniffling, eyes down, as he tried to rub the tears away.

I took his arm and pulled him out of line. "Wait, Cory, I want to talk to you."

"No, I want to go home," he sobbed.

"Go on outside," I directed the children who had stopped to watch.

"Now Cory," I said, "tell me what is bothering you."

"I just want to go home. I don't want to stay at school anymore." He dabbed at his eyes with little fists.

"I'm your friend, Cory. I have to know what your problem is before I can let you go home."

"Lucretia said she hates me," he wailed.

I put my arm around him. "Oh, Cory, you liked Lucretia, didn't you?"

I kneeled down to Cory's level. "Cory, you liked Lucretia so much that you forgot to look at the other boys and girls. All the children like you, Cory. Now you go out and find some new friends. See those kids over by the slide, Cory. They are not playing. See if they'll play shadow tag with you. Go have fun," I urged him, as I started him out the door with a little pat on the seat.

When the bell rang to end recess, I watched the children come into the hall and looked for Cory. There he was at the end of the line, finishing up a game of tag with Jan and Lucy. The little grin was back.

"That was a quick recovery from a broken heart," I mused. "Now maybe math..."

My hopes for Cory to develop a liking for school work were short lived. Now it was Lucy taking his attention. He giggled and she giggled.

"Ignore Cory, Lucy, or I will have to move him," I warned.

When Lucy studiously avoided him the rest of the day, Cory was lost. Toward the end of the day, I saw Cory holding his slate over his head, so everyone could read what he had written. I left the group I was working with and took the slate. He had written, "GRILS ARE SILLIE."

"I don't know what you mean here, Cory. You have "GRILS ARE SILLIE." Does anyone know what Cory is talking about?"

No one volunteered to explain.

"What are 'grils', Cory?"

Cory ducted his head and for five minutes he worked. The next thing Cory did was to go back to Jan's desk and drop a note on it. I went to Jan's desk and picked up the note. I stood Cory in front of the room and told him to read the note to the room. He looked at my face, searching for a sign of mercy and saw none. He burst into tears.

I kneeled down in front of Cory. "Listen to me, Cory," I said, "I don't care when you do your arithmetic, either now, or after school, but you will do it. You have only ten minutes." In seven minutes the page of arithmetic was finished, testifying to Cory's bright mind.

On Monday, a new girl came to our room. She was not only pretty, but had a magnetic personality that pulls in everyone around. It wasn't hard to pull in Cory. He was her immediate slave. Rosalee seemed unspoiled by all the attention.

On Fridays, we had been choosing a "King and Queen For A Day." They got special privileges, and it was considered a great honor. Everyone had already had a turn, so now we had been choosing someone we had seen doing a kind deed during the week. Since Rosalee had never had a turn, the children agreed that she should be "Queen For A Day." Since the boys had all had a turn, I suggested to Rosalee that she choose one. She seemed pleased and grateful to have been chosen.

She came to the front of the room and stood looking around. She looked up and down the aisles. Each boy watched her, hoping to be chosen. Cory sat there with that cute little grin on his face and seemed sure he would be chosen.

Rosalee turned to me and said, "Miss Lillie, my great-grandmother is ninety years old. She lived when Abraham Lincoln did. On my birthday last week, she gave me a card. I brought it today. May I read it?"

"Please do, Rosalee. And I'd like to meet your great-grandmother."

"Thank you, Miss Lillie. It says this: 'When you pick your friends, choose the ones who work hard, the ones who are kind, and the ones who can laugh at themselves.' I'm going to always keep this card and remember what it says. So, for "King For A Day," I'm going to pick Raymond." And she pointed to a dark-eyed boy on the front seat.

Of course, the boys were all surprised, but none more than Raymond. Cory dropped his head on his desk to pout. He lifted it a little and peered out when Rosalee began explaining her choice.

"I've been here only a week, but I've noticed Raymond never looks around, or plays around. He just works until it's all done. Then he draws pictures or reads. He carried Johnny's books this morning because Johnny fell out of a tree and sprained his arm. I don't know if he can laugh at himself or not, but maybe we can make him laugh today while he's king."

Raymond was grinning the biggest grin I'd ever seen on him. Maybe we could make him laugh.

We put the crowns on Raymond and Rosalee and sang this song to them:

> Hail to the Queen
> And hail to the King.
> This is our song,
> To them we sing.
> They will reign
> In our court today.
> They will rule
> In our work and our play.
> Hail! Hail! Hail!

I looked at Cory. He was singing heartily.

He must have survived another broken heart, I decided. I discovered that something else had happened to Cory. He was bright enough to catch what Rosalee had said. If Rosalee liked hard workers, Cory was going to be one of them. After that day, I seldom ever had to remind him to do his work. Rosalee, with the help of her great-grandmother, had accomplished what I, Miss Lillie, had failed to do. She had persuaded Cory of the importance of work.

THE SIXTEENTH PRESIDENT

I had seen the old man sitting there on the porch as I walked to school each day. One evening, he was puttering around a small patch of marigolds near the gate as I walked home, and when he looked up, I nodded a brief greeting. From then on, we said "Good morning" in the mornings and "Hello" in the evenings.

One evening, a small boy hung on the gate, swinging it back and forth, squeaking it as it went. He was a handsome little fellow, with sky-blue eyes and the blackest of lashes. I smiled, and he stopped the gate long enough to tell me, "I'm Andrew, Andrew Owens."

"And I'm Miss Lillie. Are you visiting your grandfather?"

"Yes, he's my grandpa, and he's my Mama's grandpa, too."

"Then he's your great-grandpa."

"I know he's great, 'cause he knows everything."

"He knows everything?"

"Yes, just about everything. He reads giant great big books."

"Someday you will read giant great big books, too, Andrew."

"I know. Someday I'll go to school. And I'll read when I go to school."

After that week, I didn't see the boy anymore, and the old man looked sad and lonely sitting on the porch alone. One evening when he didn't wave, I followed a strong urge and followed the path up to the porch. He was asleep in his chair with his feet perched up on the rail.

When I said "Hello", his feet dropped to the porch floor and his eyes opened wide in surprise.

"Taking a nap?" I asked.

"I must have dozed off, " he said.

We talked about the weather and the flowers, and I could see the old man was happy to visit, even for a few short minutes.

"I'm Miss Lillie," I told him. "I teach at the school."

"I figured you did," he responded. "I'm Joe Farley. People just call me Old Joe."

In the visits that followed, I learned a lot about Old Joe. He had lived an interesting life, and was content with what he had left.

One evening, I asked about the little grandson, Andrew.

"Oh, he's my pride and joy. I never get to see him though. My granddaughter and Andrew are all the family I have left."

There seemed to be some uneasiness in his tone that left me wondering. I had a feeling he hadn't told me all there was to tell.

Winter came in and the weather turned cold. I saw less and less of Old Joe. He was seldom on the porch, and when he was, I waved and went on, hurrying to get home out of the cold and into the school work I always carried home with me.

On January 20th, a big snow came, and was still coming down when I passed Old Joe's house. Hurrying along, I almost missed him standing there on the porch. I was nearly past the gate when I looked up and saw him wave from the porch. I could see he was motioning me to come in. I really wanted to hurry on home, but when I saw he had shoveled a path to the porch, I turned in and walked up to where he was standing.

"Don't you want a cup of hot cocoa?" he shouted above the sound of the wind.

I went inside, dumped my bag of books on the table, and sat down. It was warm and cheery and I was tired after walking from school against the blowing snow. Starting my second cup of cocoa, I asked about the grandson, Andrew.

"I'm worried about them," he began. I looked at Old Joe and saw an old man who carried a heavy burden of anxiety and had no one to talk to about it.

"Where are they?"

"I haven't heard from them in two months. They were

down in South Carolina, and now I don't know where they are. It's not like Lizbeth not to write."

"Have you written to her?"

"My last letter came back."

I could see Old Joe was trying hard to hide his concern.

"Why did they go to South Carolina?"

"Oh, that's where he wanted to go. I think his folks are down there."

"Her husband?"

"Well, yes. She married him after Clayton died. That's Andrew's father—now there was a good man. I never trusted this other fellow, Miss Lillie."

I could offer Joe little help, except that I listened. I left, wondering what *could* be done.

The days grew warmer, and occasionally I would see Old Joe on the porch and would wave at him. Then one day, there was little Andrew standing by the gate. He looked subdued and quiet, not quite the same child I had seen swinging on the gate a few months back.

"Hello, Andrew," I greeted him. "How are you and Grandpa?"

"Maybe I can live with Grandpa now," he stated bluntly.

Just then Old Joe came out on the porch and waved at me. I went up and sat down.

"Did Andrew and his mother come for a visit?" I asked to start the conversation.

"She's gone to the store for me, so I will tell you the story. I knew he wasn't good to them, but when he got worse, she got up early one morning, packed up her clothes and left him. She had no money, so she had to catch rides, mostly with farmers— once on a load of hay and once with pigs. They can stay with me. There's a little room upstairs we can clean up for Andrew."

"I'm glad they're here," I told him. "Now you won't have to worry about them anymore."

As I left, I spoke again to Andrew at the gate. "How old are you now, Andrew?"

"I'm almost five," he said proudly. "When I'm six, I can go to school."

Kindergartens were being started up in some of the big cities, and when our little town found extra money from a harness and boot factory that had located in town, the board decided to try it. There was great excitement among the townspeople who had children that age.

I didn't think of asking for the job, and it was a big surprise to me when the board asked me to take the new Kindergarten room. It was a big decision, as I would need to go to summer school in a nearby city for training in Kindergarten teaching.

A week before school started, I came back ready and eager. I spent a day at school decorating my room with charts and pictures. Two pictures were already there—George Washington's and Abraham Lincoln's—and I'm sure they were in every classroom in every school in the country.

On the way home from school, as I neared Old Joe's house, I remembered that his grandson, Andrew, would be old enough to start to kindergarten.

I saw them on the porch and they were both waving at me. Andrew was yelling something and I couldn't make it out until I was almost to the porch.

"I'm going to school. I'm old enough. I'm going to Kindergarten—Grandpa said so."

Old Joe laughed and I laughed, too. It was so good to see them genuinely happy.

"You surely are," I agreed. "You be sure and come to school the very first day," I urged.

"You couldn't keep him away," Joe stated.

That first year in Kindergarten was full of exciting days. With so many interesting five-year-olds, it could not be dull. One day in February still stands out in my memory—It was a great day for Andrew. We had been talking about United States' presidents. The children knew Woodrow Wilson was our president at that time, but we were just beginning to study two other presidents—the two whose pictures hung on our classroom wall—Abraham Lincoln and George Washington. Andrew seemed particulary interested in this new subject. Old Joe was quite a historian and Andrew seemed to be following in his footsteps.

The day before Lincoln's birthday, I was on my way home, when I spotted Old Joe sweeping snow from the path to his house.

"Miss Lillie," he called out, looking around to make sure Andrew wasn't nearby. "I know Andrew's a quiet boy, maybe what you'd call shy, but he just may surprise you tomorrow," he said with a sly grin.

"What do you mean?"

"Well, you know how much Andrew loves my books—especially the encyclopedias and history books."

"Yes, I know. He talks about your giant books and brags about how you know everything."

"He's the smart one—you'll see," he said, and added, "tomorrow, ask the class if anyone knows which president Abraham Lincoln was."

"I'll do that, Joe," I promised and hurried home full of anticipation for the next day.

Andrew came in just as the bell was ringing.

"Just in time, Andrew," I said, picking up the attendance sheet.

The children had learned the flag salute and we stood for that. Max, the little show-off, tried to see how fast he could say it, so we had to take a second try with my hand on Max's shoulder, and this time it came out smooth as silk.

"Now children," I announced, "today is someone's birthday. Does anyone know whose?"

"Mine! Mine! Mine!" came shouts all around the circle.

It is always interesting to watch the countenances of small children. There, if anywhere, you will find honesty. I glanced around the circle and my attention rested on Andrew. He had a small grin, seeming amused at the childrens' claim to a birthdate.

"No, not yours." I quieted them with a hand signal. "It's a famous president."

"George Washington," came shouts again.

"Children do you remember what we do before answering a question."

"We raise our hands," Max shouted, waving his hand in the air.

"All right, Max, you may answer."

"It's Abraham Lincoln," Max announced, looking around the circle proudly.

"Right, Max. It is Abraham Lincoln's birthday. Now, can anyone tell me which president he was?"

Sara, the little cutie, held up her hand. Andrew did not have his hand up and when I glanced his way he was fidgeting nervously. Grandfather is going to be disappointed, I thought.

"Sara?" I nodded to her. "Which president was Abraham Lincoln?"

"The greatest one," Sara announced, looking all around the circle with a big proud smile.

"Yes, he was a great one," I agreed, but that is not what I mean." I looked at Andrew. Still no hand up. He was intently studying the toes of his new buckskin boots his grandfather had bought for him.

"Children, let me show you what I mean. Start numbering off. Sara you say "First", Aaron say, "Second", and go on around the circle.

I could see Andrew was getting worried. He was staring hard at me when we got to sixteenth, and his whole body relaxed when we went on to seventeenth and on to twenty-third.

"Now, see what I mean children? Which number was Abraham Lincoln?"

Again, no response from Andrew, but Aaron was waving his hand wildly in the air. I thought of helping Andrew by calling on him, but I knew I should not coax him. Someday, he had to find courage, the courage that comes from within, with no outside help from anyone.

"Aaron?" I asked. I looked at Andrew and alarm was on his face.

"He was the first," Aaron answered.

"Sorry, Aaron. Not right."

Sara and Max were waving their hands frantically.

"Sara?"

"Second," Sara guessed.

"Max?"

Andrew's face was a kaleidoscope of mirrored emotions. Real anxiety was there now, as Max prepared to answer.

"Third," Max answered.

Again, Andrew's body slumped, showing relief, but still his hand was not up.

"Children, no more guessing," I told them.

At that announcement, Andrew showed real dejection, as if the game were all over. Poor Grandpa—poor Old Joe. What could I do? I looked around the circle.

"Now, if anyone thinks of the RIGHT answer and if you think you really know, hold up your hand."

I looked all around—no hands up. All eyes were on me. They were expecting me to tell them. Andrew was looking all around the circle. He looked frightened. All those eyes. Could he stand them all staring at him, as they were staring at me, the teacher? I looked around the circle, then back at Andrew for that last chance—that one last chance for him and for Old Joe. Then I saw a sudden burst of courage flood his countenance. His hand shot up—all the way up. Does he remember the right answer? Please, oh, please, Andrew, get it right.

"Andrew," I called out.

"Sixteenth, Miss Lillie. Abraham Lincoln was the sixteenth president of the United States of America," he said with pride and great relief.

"Andrew!" now I was the one shouting.

"Andrew! You are right. Abraham Lincoln WAS the sixteenth president of the United States of America. How did you know that, Andrew?"

Suddenly, Andrew was so proud of himself, he was glowing like a candle in a dark room. He looked all around the circle and saw all eyes were on him and everyone was smiling. He saw Sara smiling; he saw Aaron smiling; he saw Max smiling, and the smiles of all the others.

Again, I asked, "How did you know that, Andrew?"

"Grandpa and I read it in one of his big books."

I had all the children repeat it three times: Abraham Lincoln was the sixteenth president of the United States of America.

That evening, when I walked past Old Joe's house, he met me at the gate.

"You know, that grandson was the proudest kid I've ever seen when he came home today," he said. "Thanks, Miss Lillie. Thanks a lot."

"Thank you, Joe," I responded.

"With a great-grandfather like you to back him, I think Andrew Owens is going to do all right."

CARROT-TOP REDHEAD

"Shall I put down her real name, Miss Lillie? We never call her that at home." Bonnie, the middle Johnson girl, paused with her pencil in the air. We had never had enrollment forms before, but this year the county superintendent had asked for them. Bonnie was filling out the form for her little sister.

"Put down her real name, of course, Bonnie."

"I'll put it down, but don't call her that. She doesn't like it."

"Write down the name you call her, too. Put them both down."

"Well, her real name is Lucinda Suzanne," Bonnie explained, but we call her Cindy Sue." I could see that Bonnie was off on one of her long rambling tales, and on the first morning of school, I didn't have time to listen.

"She's named for my two grandmothers, and do you know why?" Bonnie didn't wait for an answer. "Cindy Sue has red hair, orangey-red hair, and so do my two grandmothers."

"What! Are you saying that both your grandmothers have red hair?"

Bonnie was elated that she had piqued my interest. "Yes, both grandmothers. And both Grandma Harris and Grandma Johnson each think that Cindy Sue got her red hair from her. Mama says they're kinda jealous of each other. They were always buying things for Cindy Sue until Mama and Papa told them to quit. We girls were spoiling her, too until Mama told us to quit waiting on her."

"Good for your Mama," I responded.

Before Bonnie could add more to the family background, Virgil Johnson came in, holding a little girl by the hand. I knew without introduction that it must be Cindy Sue. Orangey-red hair, indeed! Her head was covered with orangey-red ringlets. Her blue eyes looked around quizzically, taking it all in, then settled on me, with a look that clearly said, "I'm not sure I'm going to like you." She was a truly beautiful child with skin the texture of thin white porcelain, highlighted by a faint color of pink roses in her cheeks, and a sprinkle of freckles across her tiny nose.

I greeted Mr. Johnson and smiled down at Cindy Sue, getting no smile in return. Bonnie took her hand and guided her over to the first grade seats.

"We're slow this year, Miss Lillie." Virgil Johnson apologized. "If I could get a book list for the girls, I'll go pick them up today. My wife's mother's been sick and I been sowin' wheat, but we're gettin' caught up now." He glanced back at Cindy Sue. "Miss Lillie," he confided in a low tone, "You'll find her a lot different from her sisters. She's got a temper like a wildcat. I guess maybe we spoiled her because she's our youngest."

"Don't worry. We'll get along." I assured him.

A few days went by uneventfully, as Cindy Sue and all the others settled into the routine of a school day. On Friday of the second week, I was finishing my lunch and grading papers when I heard yelps coming from the playground. When I went to check, I found Danny, a third grade boy, on the ground with Cindy Sue on top of him, flailing away at him with little fists. Danny was kicking and pushing, trying to upset her. He was trying to stifle his cries, as it would not enhance his image among the boys if they saw a first grade girl had downed him.

"Cindy Sue," I called to her three times before she stopped pummeling Danny and looked up at me. "Cindy Sue, come into the schoolhouse. You, too, Danny." Inside the schoolroom, the children sat on the reading bench beside my desk, staring at me.

"Cindy Sue, why were you hitting Danny?"

"He called me 'old carrot-top redhead', and he said I was ugly," and Cindy Sue burst into tears.

"Oh, Cindy Sue," I comforted her, gathering her onto my

lap. "Danny, how could you? Cindy Sue is very pretty." She raised her head and looked at me through the fingers that covered her face.

"Danny, what do you have to say?"

"I'm sorry, and I sure won't call her that again."

"Well, I hope not. Her name is Cindy Sue, and I've always liked red hair."

"And, Cindy Sue, what can you say to Danny?"

"I won't punch him again," she promised.

Cindy Sue slid off my lap. Danny took her hand. "I'll push you in the swing," he offered, and that was the beginning of a lasting friendship.

The day before Thanksgiving, we were playing baseball at the noon recess. The first graders were pig-tailing the outfield, and a grounder rolled to a stop between Cindy Sue and Patricia. Both girls rushed to get it, and Patricia picked it up a split second before Cindy Sue reached for it. Patricia threw the ball in, then Cindy Sue tackled her. When I reached them, Patricia was screaming as Cindy Sue struck her again and again. I pulled the little redhead off, and stood her beside me, then helped Patricia to her feet.

"Why did you do that, Cindy Sue?" I asked angrily.

"I was supposed to get the ball," Cindy Sue wailed.

"No, Cindy Sue, whoever reaches it first is suppose to get it. Go sit on the porch steps and think about it," I ordered. "Patricia, go wash your face and get back into the game."

Cindy Sue had accepted me as a friend, and now she felt angry and deserted. As she stomped off, I watched her go, feeling a little guilty. When she was halfway to the schoolhouse, I saw her fall. She sprawled out on the ground, and I supposed she had stumbled. When I realized she wasn't getting up, I raced to her. The children left the game and followed me. As I reached down to pick her up, a stern voice commanded, "Don't touch her Miss Lillie; leave her alone."

I looked up at Cindy Sue's two sisters. Amanda, the eighth grader was speaking. "Miss Lillie, Papa said he should have told you, but we thought Cindy Sue was over these temper fits she used to have. You see, Grandma Johnson kept her for three months when she was two years old. That's when Mama was sick. She pulled these temper tantrums to get anything she wanted. When she came home, we took her to Dr. Dilling, and he didn't find anything wrong with her. He said to try ignoring her. We did, and it worked. Please, Miss Lillie, she's just trying you out. Let's go back to the game."

"All right, if you say so," I agreed reluctantly. I remembered her pale face and closed eyes, and glanced over at big sister Amanda. Her countenance appeared adamant. I wasn't sure how I was calling the game, for my eyes were on the little figure lying on the grass, halfway to the schoolhouse door.

It was probably not more than five minutes after Cindy Sue had fallen, that I saw her raise her head, look around, get up, and walk off. As she sat down on the steps, Amanda, big sister, turned to me and grinned. We had won the day.

Two weeks before school closed, it suddenly turned summer. That morning in May found us opening windows that had been closed since October. At noon, the children left their shoes and stockings at the schoolhouse door, and raced for the creek. There in the shade of willow and cottonwood, they splashed in the sandy-bottomed stream that ran just beyond the school yard. With a sandwich in one hand and an apple in the other, they enjoyed life at its best.

"A turtle!" yelled Sammy.

"A frog, a green frog," sang back Christy.

I stood on the bank and watched. "Guess I'll get my lunch and sit on the bank," I mused.

"Come on in," Damien invited.

"Maybe tomorrow," I called back.

"A white bird! Miss Lillie! A white bird! Around the bend there. What is it?"

I looked up the creek. "A heron, I think," I called back. "Look it up when you get back into the schoolroom."

I was reluctant to ring the one o'clock bell, but finally did at one-fifteen. The afternoon, slow and lazy, finally ended. At four o'clock, there was only one missing stocking, and I found it under the heating stove after they'd all started home. I was hanging it on a nail in the cloak room, when a movement at

the girl's outhouse caught my attention. I stepped out of sight and peered from behind the door. Maybe it was a stray dog, but I didn't think so.

Then out of the outhouse who should emerge but little Carrot-top Redhead. She looked around to be sure she was safe, then scooted across the playground toward home.

I was puzzled. If she had to use the outhouse, why hadn't her sisters waited for her? It was then that I remembered that Amanda and Bonnie had stayed home to help because their mother had a new baby, and they were going to do lessons at home for a week.

"Cindy Sue," I called. "Why aren't you on your way home?"

Cindy Sue stopped in her tracks, the picture of guilt. I knew something unusual had taken her to the outhouse. She stood stock-still staring at the ground.

"Cindy Sue, you can tell me," I encouraged. "It can't be that bad."

She raised her misery-laden face. "You won't tell my Mama?"

"I don't know, Cindy Sue. I don't know if I can promise that. If it's not too awful bad, I guess I can promise."

"It's bad," Cindy Sue confessed gravely, "but I guess I'll have to tell you." She hesitated, took a deep breath, and made a brave start. "When the kids all took off their shoes and stockings at noon, I couldn't take mine off because I still had on my long underwear. My Mama told me I had to wear my winter underwear until it got really hot. It was really hot today, wasn't it, Miss Lillie?" She looked at me uncertainly. "I had to come out here to take them off. I hid them under the catalogs. I had to come out after school to put them back on. Are you going to tell my Mama? She stood there with a worried look on her face.

"No, I won't tell her. Cross my heart and hope to die," I promised solemnly. "Now hurry, and you can catch the other children down the road."

Cindy Sue breathed a sigh of relief, grinned happily, and raced down the road toward home.

I'M YOUR KID, REMEMBER ME?

Because of an appendix surgery that fall, I had been unable to start the school year. In the little town nearby, I could substitute for anyone who needed me. My wages would be one or two dollars a day, and would be paid by the teacher.

One day in late December, I found myself in Primary I for a teacher who had pneumonia. As I looked around the room that morning, one face stood out in the sea of little faces. There was something about him—some tender bit of magnetism that drew my attention. He had a faint aura of sweet yearning, as if to indicate he had been loved, but had also known neglect. His clothes fit the picture, well-worn, but adequate. The blue Scout shirt had three merit badges and a rip on the pocket. He sat twiddling his pencil.

"Need help on the arithmetic?" I asked. "I'll help you as soon as I get the reading class started."

"He's new. His name's Lexie," Johnny offered.

"Well, you and I are both new to this room, Lexie. I'm the substitute for today." I turned to Johnny. "Give him a little help until I get back," I suggested. I stopped at the desk to look at his enrollment form. "New York City", it said.

My thoughts returned to Lexie as I worked on the reading class. Those deep blue eyes fringed with black lashes harbored a subtle loneliness that made you want to reach out to him; yet he had an air of independence that comes naturally to one who has had to adjust early to life's inequities. He seemed to grasp the principles on the number page quickly and was quietly working away when the bell rang for morning recess.

Even in good weather, I did not relish playground duty, and today was anything but good. The wind was howling down from the Colorado Rockies onto the Kansas Plains. "The playground would have to be located on the north side of the building," I mused, ducking my head further down into my scarf and collar. It was a long fifteen minutes, but finally the return bell rang. As I started toward the building, I noticed a little bundled-up figure walking beside me. "Come on," I shouted, above the wind's roar. "Let's get inside before we freeze."

At the door he opened it, and stepped back for me to enter. "Thank you, sir. What room are you in?" I thought I would put in a good word to his teacher for his show of courtesy.

"I'm yours. I'm your kid. Remember me?" he exclaimed, as he pulled off his scarf and threw back his cap. I recognized Lexie in those deep blue eyes and that friendly smile.

"Sure, Lexie, I know you. I just couldn't see you. You had your head covered."

"I'm your kid. Remember me?" ran through my mind as I finished out the day of teaching.

The second day in the room, I was to practice the children on their Christmas program. We found a place in the play for Lexie. After school, there was Lexie, still hanging around, trying to help with the decorations and asking questions.

"Will there be a Christmas tree?" he asked.

"I think someone is suppose to pick one up this evening. I've heard they always have one."

"Last year, we didn't get to have a tree. Santa forgot us." I looked at Lexie. I could see his thoughts were far away, as he stood there twirling a paper chain around his finger. His face was an expression of sadness, and he seemed to be lost in thoughts of another time, another place.

I wanted to jar him out of his mood. "Lexie, believe me, Santa will not forget you this year."

Lexie smiled, and the sadness drained from his face.

I was nearly ready to go home when Zachary Wheeler stepped in. "I'm going after the Christmas tree, and if you're

54

ready to go home, tell me where you want me to put it."

"At one end of the stage in that big room with all the seats. How long will you be?"

"A good half hour. It's at Kelly's farm."

"Could we wait, Miss Lillie, so I can see it?" Lexie's eyes were shining bright as two stars. I couldn't say, "no".

"We'll wait if you're sure your mother won't care."

"My mother doesn't care where I am," Lexie said flatly.

"Why not let the kid come? I've got my two boys in the wagon."

"If you're sure your mother won't worry, Lexie."

After they left, I swept the room, and started grading papers. Zachary Wheeler was correct on estimating the time, for in exactly a half hour, I saw them drive in. I heard Mr. Wheeler yell "Whoa", then I heard someone else yelling. I went to the window and saw Mr. Wheeler kneeling beside the wagon. One boy had jumped out, and was holding the horses, and the other was climbing over the sideboard.

Zachary Wheeler had picked up a bundle from the ground and was coming toward the schoolhouse. I saw legs dangling. It had to be Lexie. I rushed down the hall and met them at the door.

"He fell out of the wagon just before we stopped. Zack Jr. said he was sitting on the sideboard, and when we turned, it threw him off. His head must have struck the wheel, or maybe the frozen ground."

Lexi's eyes were closed in a face as white as chalk. His body hung limp.

I handed Zack Jr. a cloth. "Go get this wet and put it on his forehead. Lay him on this table, Mr. Wheeler. I'll try to find a phone and call the doctor. I was sure his mother didn't have a phone.

In the office, I called the town's only doctor, but he was out. I rushed back to the room. Lexie lay there, still white and lifeless.

"He's breathing all right, " Mr. Wheeler told me. Zack Jr. had put the cloth on his forehead. I handed him a pan and sent him for more cold water. When he came back, we bathed

56

his face. I remembered Lexie's words from the first day I was in Primary I Room.

"I'm your kid. Remember me?"

Now I prayed silently: "Dear God, Lexie is your kid. Remember him. Please bring him back to us."

Anxiously, I watched his face. I thought I saw an eyelid flutter. Could I have imagined it? Then both eyelids fluttered visibly and the next thing I knew, his eyes were open, and he was looking at me. He looked on beyond me, and around the room with a dazed expression on his pale face.

"Where am I?" he asked.

"You fell out of the wagon, son," Zachary Wheeler told him. "You bumped your head and it knocked you out."

"Where is the Christmas tree?" he asked.

"It's in the wagon and we'll bring it in, now that you're going to be all right. How do you feel?"

"I feel all right," Lexie told him, as he started to get up.

"Lie still a few minutes," I told him. "Pretty soon, if you feel like it, you can sit up and see the tree."

Zachary Wheeler had been mighty relieved to see Lexie come to. He and Zachary Jr. brought in the big tree and set it up in a tub of wet sand. Lexie was sitting up now, watching the tree with big eyes. "It's a beautiful tree, Mr. Wheeler," I told him.

"It'll look real purty with candles on it, " Zachary Wheeler said. "That's a picture that always sends shivers up my spine."

"It will be pretty, but I've heard this is the last year we can put candles on it."

"Why?" Mr. Wheeler asked.

"It's just not safe, Mr. Wheeler. It can start a fire. Tomorrow all the children in the school will decorate the tree."

"Me, too?" asked Lexie.

"You too, Lexie."

"Did you say there'd be candy on the tree?"

"I've heard it's so," I told him, "and maybe a little toy for everyone."

I decided for sure there would be something for Lexie.

Lexie was up walking around when Mr. Wheeler and the boys got ready to go.

"You come on, Lexie," Mr. Wheeler invited. "I'm going to see you get home without any more accidents."

"Thanks, Mr. Wheeler."

"Good-bye, Miss Lillie. I'll help you decorate the Christmas tree tomorrow."

THE TRANSFORMATION OF BUTCHIE

That year in first grade was like any other year, except there was Francie. If I live to be a thousand, I shall never forget Francie, Francie Felersen. Golden curls framed her face like a halo, a face that had a strange happy glow that made you think of Springtime and birdsong. Yet there were times when her face was a picture of sadness, and strangely, when she was sad, the sadness was reflected in everyone around her.

Francie's mother had reared three children, and now she lavished her skill with a needle on Francie, designing dresses with ruffles and laces and frills. All the little girls gravitated toward her and the little boys adored her, but she remained as unspoiled as a blossoming rose.

"Her parents must feel fortunate to have such a perfect child," Joyce Kramer told me. "And you should feel lucky to have her in your room. But then, you have Butchie." Joyce taught across the hall, and we shared school problems.

Yes, there was Butchie, the new boy. He hadn't been with us long until he had bullied and bluffed everyone into being afraid of him, everyone except Francie. Butchie didn't seem to see Francie; he was too busy pushing the other children around.

As Summer started to fade into Autumn, the children brought beetles to school, beetles and grasshoppers and garter snakes. They brought them in jars with holes punched in the lids, boxes with screen on top, and in bottles. Butchie brought a horned-toad in his pocket, which took us on a search to get help on the proper habitat and food for the little lizard.

I noticed that Francie brought nothing to the collection on

the science table. Her mother remarked one morning, "She can stand motionless watching a butterfly sunning on a twig, or watch an ant carrying his treasure back to his den, but she never touches them."

"Well, some children are a little squeamish about handling insects or reptiles," I explained.

"Oh, I don't think she's loathe to touch them," her mother responded. "She just respects them."

That afternoon it rained, and recess was inside. Some children gathered around the science table. Butchie, as usual, jostled someone out of the way to find a space for himself near the table. Francie stood nearby, silently eyeing the jars and boxes.

"Let them go," I heard her say. "They are not happy shut up."

A child started some lively music on the record player,

and soon everyone was skipping around the room.

"Let them go; let them go; let them go," Francie started chanting, and everyone joined her in the chant.

After recess, we read poetry and decided to write some of our own. "I can't write no poems," Butchie muttered as he went back to the blocks. I copied down the poetic thoughts of each child as they were told to me. Francie wrote her own and wanted to read it to the room.

"Mine rhymes," she announced, apparently happy with her efforts, as she began to read.

> "Please open up the jar;
> Let it fly away so far;
> Let it go.
> It wants to be free,
> Just the same as you and me;
> Let it go."

"Wonderful, Francie. What a good poem," I encouraged her.

"Wow! That's a really good poem," Butchie said, surprising everyone.

I reminded the children of refrains, and asked how Francie could use one. Again, Butchie surprised us.

"Let it go; let it go; let it go;" he called out.

Now a jubilant Francie read it again, as Butchie sat beaming at the thought of having contributed to it.

> "Please open up the jar;
> Let it fly away so far;
> Let it go; let it go; let it go;
>
> It wants to be free,
> Just the same as you and me;
> Let it go; let it go; let it go."

Francie was happy at the children's "Oohs" and "Ahs," and for the next few days, she was frequently at my elbow with a new poetic effort.

On Friday of that week, Butchie brought a dead baby squirrel to school after he saw a Model T hit it. We put it in a shoebox coffin and buried it in the corner of Archie's yard across from the school. After the burial, the children raced off to play, all but Francie. She sat alone on the schoolhouse steps. One by one the girls joined her. Curious, I walked over to the steps and found them all either sniffling or looking miserably sad. To break the mood, we went inside and dug out the cornpopper, made popcorn, and played games for a while.

In mid-October, we came out to the playground for our last recess to see black smoke billowing into the sky northwest of the school toward downtown. The children crowded around me.

"What is it, Miss Lillie? What's burning?"

Mr. Jessup, the janitor, came out to sweep gravel off the walk.

"What is it, Mr. Jessup?" I called.

"Radio says it's an old warehouse downtown. Sure hope they head it off before it catches something else. Those sparks are flyin' right up to the sky."

The children didn't play much, but stood around watching the smoke boiling into the sky and seeing an occasional burst of flame. When the bell rang, we trooped into the building. I hadn't missed Francie and I was surprised to see her sitting quietly at her desk.

"Why are you inside on such a nice day, Francie? Are you OK?" I looked down and saw tears. "Francie, what is wrong? Why are you crying?"

"Miss Lillie," she began, her voice quivering with emotion, "the fire is going up to the sky. Mr. Jessup said so. I'm afraid it will burn up Jesus."

"Oh, Francie, that will never happen," I assured her. "The sky is a million miles away. And anyway, no fire can hurt Jesus."

"Are you sure?" she asked, wiping her eyes.

"Sure, I'm sure. Now you go feed the goldfish. I think they are hungry."

The weeks that followed brought no improvement in Butchie. It was a big worry, as the other children were beginning to resent him. I went to visit his home one evening and found that he was living with an aunt and uncle. Luckily Butchie was playing at the neighbors, so it didn't take them long to tell the story. Butchie's mother had died when he was three. His father had started drinking, and one day, he had taken Butchie to the neighbor's house and walked away.

"Since he came to us, we have tried to get close to him," Butchie's Aunt Mary said.

"I suppose Butchie is a nickname," I said. "What is his given name?"

"William Worthington Woolcott," Uncle John answered.

"Maybe he'd act differently if we called him William, or Billie, or Bill," I suggested.

"No, we asked him, and he was very resolute about it. 'My name is Butchie,' he told us," Aunt Mary explained.

The next day, I moved Butchie's desk close to mine for two

reasons: I could keep an eye on him and keep his anger from being aimed at one of the other children; and I could try to win him over. Sometimes, in explaining something to him, I would attempt to touch him on the arm or hair or shoulder, but he would pull away from me. I was getting nowhere with him.

One day, at the bell to end recess, a hard wind blowing out of the southwest seemed to blow the children across the playground right up to the door. The children bunched up at the door, and as usual, Butchie started pushing and shoving. His new baseball cap fell off his head and Archie stepped on it. Butchie turned to Archie with murder in his eye. Francie, seeing only that Butchie's cap was on the walk, picked it up and handed it to him. Her golden curls were blowing about and her face was flushed from running in the wind. She smiled that sweet smile of hers and Butchie melted. At first, his expression went blank, then changed to a look I had never seen on Butchie, a look of angelic bliss.

We stopped at the drinking fountain, and Butchie stood transfixed, staring at Francie. The other children were not aware of the transformation in Butchie, and I wondered how long it would last.

Finally, Butchie moved into line at the fountain and I heard him whisper to Archie, "She smiled at me."

"Who smiled at you?" Archie asked aloud.

"Shut up, Stupid," Butchie said in an undertone, but I noticed he was still smiling. "It was Francie. Francie smiled at me."

"So what?" Archie verbally jabbed at him. "She smiles at everyone."

This did not dampen Butchie's spirits, and I was so happy to see Butchie transformed, that I did not mind seeing him sitting there staring at Francie the rest of the day instead of doing his work.

The days that followed were peaceful ones. Butchie's personality had indeed changed. He needed help in working out his new relationship with the children, but soon he was taking turns, giving in, and making friends.

One day we studied capital letters and names. The

66

children wrote down their full names and read them to the class. Archie was Archibald Lynn Hunter; Beth was Elizabeth Suzanne Sampson; and Colen was Colen Lee Combs. Francie read her name, "Francene Marghretta Felersen." Each time a child read the full name, there were "Oohs" and "Ahs."

I wondered about Butchie. I wondered if he knew how to write his full name. But he did. He stood up and read in an undertone, as if he were embarrassed of his name.

"I can't hear him," came complaints from all over the room.

"Read it louder for the children, Butchie. I didn't hear you either," I suggested.

Butchie's head was still down. Then he lifted it just enough to peer around the room. All eyes were on him. It was too much. He sat down.

"Butchie?" I said.

"I don't want to," he answered, his head still down.

"OK, Butchie, I'll read it for you. Bring it here."

Butchie laid his paper on my desk.

When he was seated, I read it, "William Worthington Woolcott."

"Wow!" someone said in awe.

Butchie took it as ridicule and turned in anger, his first show of belligerence since the day Francie smiled at him. I knew I needed to diffuse his anger, but Francie was ahead of me.

"That's a really good name, Butchie. I like that name. My grandfather's name is William. He always reads me stories, and once he read me a story about a king named William. He jokes and tells me he's that king."

Everyone laughed and Butchie's pride was restored. Again, I saw something new in Butchie, a happiness, a peace, and at the same time a puzzlement, as if he did not know how he really felt or why.

Winter was almost over when Asian 'Flu came into town. The hospitals were full and whole families were down with it. Over fifty percent of the school children were out of school. I escaped, and Butchie, too, was one of the lucky ones. He wasn't very happy though. He and Archie were now best of pals, and Archie was absent from school along with Francie.

"When are they comin' back, Miss Lillie," he asked a hundred times. "How long does 'flu make you sick?"

The children started drifting back to school, and Butchie was happy to see Archie. Every day, though, he asked, "When is Francie comin' back?"

One evening, I came through the door of my rooming house to find the telephone ringing. It was Francie's Aunt Minnie. "Miss Lillie," she began "The news on Francie is not good. She had double pneumonia, and she's very low."

"Oh, no," was all I could say. I was shocked at the news. The children were recovering and coming back to school. Why couldn't Francie?

"Well, Miss Lillie, we've known it might end this way. When Francie was born, she had defective lungs. The doctors warned us then that she might not live beyond eight years. This 'flu hit her hard and the doctor doesn't think she can pull through."

"I'm sorry," I said lamely. I couldn't even think of my room without Francie.

"You must understand this, Miss Lillie, we are not surprised or shocked. We've lived with this for seven years. We are just thankful we had her this long. We have good memories. She's always been so special to us."

"And to me, to us, to all of us at school," I answered.

How could I explain this at school? I didn't think I could. I thought of Butchie—poor Butchie. How can I ever explain it— was all that came to my mind.

The next day at school, I told only part of it. "Francie is very sick," I said. "Maybe if we make a giant greeting card, it will cheer her up. I can take it up after school. We'll take turns painting on this big piece of paper."

"I'll make mine funny," Butchie said. "Maybe she'll laugh and get well."

After school, Butchie hung around. "Butchie, go home and ask Aunt Mary if you can help me take the greeting card up to Francie," I suggested.

68

He was happy for the first time in many days, and we were soon going through the door at the hospital. Suddenly, I regretted having asked Butchie to go. I knew Francie would not look like the little girl Butchie had known. Would he figure out the truth? Why hadn't I put it off? I looked down at him. A subdued, almost frightened look had replaced the look of happy anticipation. Maybe he had never been in a hospital before.

We hesitated at the door. Francie's mother saw us and motioned for us to come in. All too soon, we stood by the bed. Francie seemed to be asleep, and although the room was semi-dark, we could see her pale face and the golden curls falling over the pillow. I looked at Butchie. His face looked strangely pale too in the dim light of the hospital room.

"Francie," her mother said softly, "Can you wake up? Some friends are here to see you."

Francie half-opened her eyes, evidencing her weakness, but when she saw us, her eyes opened wide, and a faint smile lighted her face.

"Francie, we brought you a card from all the children." Butchie and I unrolled the big greeting card, and her face seemed to glow faintly in the dim light.

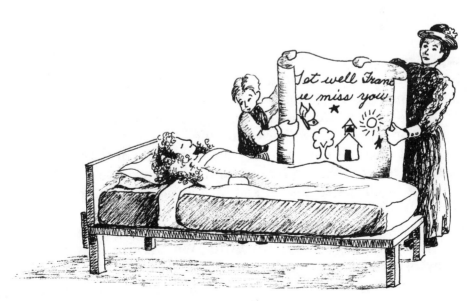

"We can't stay, Francie, for we want you to rest. We'll go now and we'll come back soon."

Butchie reached into his pocket and brought out a small tin soldier. "Here, Francie," he said. "You can have this." He placed it in her limp hand and her fingers closed over it.

A week later, on a Friday, school was let out for half a day for the funerals of Francie and a high school boy, Jerry Miller. The children and I sat together at Francie's funeral. Butchie wouldn't sit with us, but sat with his Aunt Mary.

On Monday, Butchie was not in school, and I was worried. In the evening, his Aunt Mary called me. "Butchie says he's not coming back to school anymore," she told me. "I've talked myself out. I'm worried about him. He's taking this real hard."

"I'll be over tomorrow after school," I told her. "I'd come this evening, but I have a meeting."

Tuesday evening, his aunt met me at the door. "He's out in the back," she told me. "Go on through the house."

Outside, Butchie sat on the back steps. I sat down beside him.

"We missed you at school today, Butchie." Butchie sat silent.

"Butchie, won't you come back tomorrow?"

"I'm not comin' back," he stated flatly, staring out across the yard. Butchie looked at me, then dropped his eyes.

"I went to school today, Butchie, and Francie's seat was empty. I was very unhappy. I looked at your seat and it was empty, too. Then I was so very, very unhappy, so lonesome. Not just Francie's seat, but Butchie's seat. If you don't come back, I don't want to go back either. Then who will teach the children? And the children miss you, too, Butchie. Archie misses you. Please come back, Butchie."

All at once, Butchie was crying, crying his heart out. I put my arm around him and he buried his head in my lap. After a while he lifted his tear-streaked face and looked at me. "Why do people have to die and go away?" he asked. "Why did she have to die, Miss Lillie? Kids ain't supposed to die."

"I don't know why, Butchie. We all die sometime. Everything and everybody dies sometime. Usually it's old people, sometimes it's young people, and sometimes it's even children. We just have to remember the good times we had with Francie."

"I won't ever forget her," Butchie said quietly, as he wiped his eyes.

"I'll see you in that seat at school tomorrow, Butchie," I said, as I got up to go.

The next morning, I looked out across the playground. Butchie stood alone by the fence. The bell rang, the children came in, and Butchie was sitting there in his seat again, back there by Archie, where he had asked to be moved the week before. I was at my desk, checking Archie's homework. I looked up and my eyes met Butchie's. I raised my hand in salute. Butchie's sad little face looked back at me. He hesitated, then he lifted his hand in answer.

And the day moved on.

MATILDA'S BLOOMERS

Matilda came running around the corner of the house, scooted across the yard, and shinnied up a tree.

"Matilda should have been my boy and Archie my girl," Martha Hartley told her mother-in-law. "Look how she's dressed. An old pair of Archie's overalls."

"Don't worry about her," Grandma Hartley advised her. "As I recall, I was a bit of a tomboy; then at twelve, I started paying attention to dresses and braids."

"And she's so emotional," Martha continued, as she finished shelling the peas from the garden. "She can cry one minute and laugh the next. She does well in school, except that she's always in trouble."

"And I say don't worry about her. She has a wholesome attitude toward life."

"Perhaps you're right." Martha picked up the pan of peas and started to go inside. "Now you stay out here and relax in the porch swing where it's cool. I'm going inside to see if the cream is sour enough to churn. I think I'm about out of butter."

As Martha went inside, Grandma Hartley looked up from stringing green beans to see two boys and a girl run around the house looking for Matilda who was still hidden in the tree. "Tell Matilda to come down out of that tree and come in and practice piano," Martha called from the kitchen. "She has a lesson at three."

"I'll bet that little tomboy will like that," Grandma muttered to herself.

Strangely enough, Matilda did like her music, especially the pieces with gusto. Soon her grandmother was surprised to hear Matilda's rendition of "March of the Tin Soldiers".

A Saturday picnic and Sunday church took up Matilda's weekend, then it was Monday and school again. Although the school year was almost over, Matilda still had not figured out her teacher. Some days, Miss Mattie seemed jolly and friendly, but on other days, she seemed cold and far away. For the most part, Matilda did not like school; she had to sit still too long.

She was always getting into trouble at school, so Papa had said he would buy her a pony if she could stay out of trouble. She had asked for a pony every birthday and every Christmas and many times in between, ever since the day she visited Uncle Oscar's farm and rode the Shetland pony when she was three.

There was a pony on the farm at Clay's Corner that was for sale. Papa's friend Harvey said he wanted to sell it. She heard Harvey tell Papa that it was part Shetland, part Arabian, and part Indian Paint. Every time they took the buggy out for a Sunday drive, they always went past Clay's Corner, and the pony was usually out under the trees nibbling grass with the other horses.

Once he was close to the fence and looking right at them. "He's looking at me!" Matilda had shouted. "Is not. Is looking at me," Archie had teased. Matilda had asked Papa to stop to see if they could get close enough to pet him, but Papa wouldn't stop.

The day after her birthday, she started to school looking neat and pretty in her new blue plaid dress. Her mother had combed her hair back into two neat braids with a small blue bow on each braid and a large bow on top. Matilda slipped back into the house and hid the big bow under her pillow. She knew her mother was busy getting wash water from the cistern on the back porch.

She met Jessica at the corner and they skipped happily to school. Jessica had always been her best friend. They could play together for hours and never quarrel.

At noon, Jessica wanted to roll hoops with the girls, but Matilda was engrossed in a water fight going on between two big boys at the school well.

"They'll get into trouble," Jessica warned as she walked away, starting her hoop across the playground.

Watching the water fight made Matilda thirsty. She ran into the schoolhouse, got her folding aluminum cup from her desk and came outside to the pump. A third boy pumped as the two boys threw water, and Matilda caught a cupful and drank. Some cold water splashed on her and it felt good on that hot day. She got a second cupful and casually tossed it into the air. It hit one of the boys in the face and he responded with a cupful in her face. She laughed and took aim with another cupful. When she noticed a big can sitting beside the pump, she picked it up and held it under the spout, all the time getting soaked. She could really get them with this big can of water. She raised up quickly and threw the can of water with all her might.

The boys were gone. Where had they gone? And standing in front of her was someone in trousers, a white shirt, and a tie, and from the stern face to the polished shoes, water was dripping all over him. She put the can down by the pump and picked up her drinking cup. As she folded it up, she said in a voice that was barely audible, "I'm sorry, Mr. Chandler."

Matilda spent the rest of the noon hour sitting in the principal's office. No one was there but her, so she had lots of time to think. Mr. Chandler hadn't said much to her, which was worse than a bawling out. A spanking would have been best of all, as it always paid off the debt, and left you feeling evened out again.

Mr. Chandler came in at the noon hour and sat down behind his desk. He wrote a note, sealed it in an envelope, and handed it to her. "Give this to your father," he said gravely.

Matilda walked slowly to her room. "Why do I always get mixed up in things like this?" she moaned. "Now I'll never get my pony," she thought. "Why do I always get into trouble?"

Papa was as bad Mr. Chandler. He didn't say much, just sent her to bed without her supper. That didn't bother her much, as she knew Archie would sneak some supper to her some time during the evening. What did bother her was how sad her mother looked and how disappointed Papa sounded.

She promised herself that she would never ever break any rules again.

Matilda did well for three days, and that was a record for her. On the fourth day, she sat at her desk doing her math paper when she heard, "S—s—s—s-t". She turned her head and saw Nate trying to hand her a note. She shook her head "no" and continued to work. Then a note landed on her desk; Nate had tossed it. It was folded up and on the top was the name Jessica. A note to her best friend. Somehow she'd have to give it to her. She looked at Jessica's desk, three rows over. She looked at her teacher. Miss Mattie was busy grading papers. Matilda pitched the note onto the desk beside her.

"Matilda," came that dreaded voice. "Come here."

It wouldn't do to try to explain to Papa that she just passed a note; that she didn't write it, because it was against the rules to pass notes. Slowly, reluctantly, she got out of her seat and walked toward the teacher's desk. Matilda felt a consuming anger at Nate. Why had he picked her to pass the note?

The teacher did not look up as Matilda stopped at her desk. She pointed to a score on her test paper. "Look, Matilda," she said, "a perfect score on yesterday's test, the only one in the whole room."

Matilda heaved a deep sigh. "Thank you, Miss Mattie," she said in a weak voice. Miss Mattie would never know why Matilda was so thankful. Papa had said, "The next time you deliberately break school rules, you are never to mention a pony to me again."

With only one more week of school left, Matilda was getting really excited about summer and the thought of having her very own pony.

"Horses are the absolute most beautiful creatures on earth," she had told Jessica. "So elegant, so graceful, so—so—so regal."

"So regal?" Jessica asked.

"So everything," Matilda explained.

It was on a Monday, and Matilda was eating lunch on a grassy spot back of the school building in the shade of two big locust trees. Mama had told her she could take her lunch the last week of school instead of coming home at noon, so she could eat with the children who came into town from the country. Those who were close walked, some rode horses, and the farthest ones rode into town in the kid-wagons. Mama had wanted to buy her a lunch pail at the Five and Ten, but Matilda wanted to carry her lunch in a syrup bucket like all the country kids did. Jessica was taking her lunch, too.

After finishing lunch, the children lined their lunch pails up beside the school building and raced off to play. Matilda was thrilled to have more time to play, and she stood still and looked around to see what was going on. Up at the north end, some of the big boys were playing basketball, and some were playing field hockey. Most of the younger boys were down on their knees shooting marbles, and the girls were doing jacks. It was too hot to play Tag or Foggy Over The River. At the old carriage building, four children were playing Ante-Over.

Matilda and her friends decided to play Dare Base. Well into the game, Matilda was running from dare base to home when she tripped over something and fell. She tried to get up and tumbled again. She looked down and saw that her bloomers had fallen down around her feet. She got up carefully, pulled them up to her knees, and looked around her in confusion and dismay.

"Jessica!" she called out. "Girls! Help! Help!"

The girls came running. "What's wrong? What's the matter?" they asked, crowding around her.

"My bloomers feel down. I think the elastic broke. What shall I do?"

"I know." Jessica offered. "You hold them up and we'll all make a circle around you. We'll go to the outhouse, and you can stay there while someone goes to the schoolhouse for a safety pin."

The girls joined hands and made a circle around Matilda, then they all moved slowly and awkwardly toward the outhouse. Once safe in the outhouse, they all laughed with relief.

"Penny, go and get a safety pin, and hurry," Matilda pleaded.

78

Penny was a sweet, quiet, shy little girl. She ran out of the outhouse with all the girls shouting, "Hurry, Penny, hurry."

Penny had not been gone three minutes when the bell rang.

"What am I going to do?" Matilda pleaded. "Someone stay with me."

"We have to go, Matilda," Jessica told her. "We'll get into trouble."

And away they all went, leaving Matilda very much alone. She felt deserted and frightened. She stood there waiting. The minutes seemed like hours. Why hadn't Penny come back? Where could she be? Why was it taking so long?

Back in the room, Penny sat still in her seat, too shy to speak up. She had tried. She had stood at Miss Mattie's desk waiting for her attention, but afraid to speak. Finally the teacher had said, "Everyone sit down; the bell rang ten minutes ago." And shy little Penny had silently taken her seat.

Jessica and the other girls looked at each other puzzled. They knew they should do something for poor Matilda, but they were frightened and didn't know what to do.

Miss Mattie noticed that Matilda was not in her seat. "Where's Matilda?" she asked.

No one answered. How could they say it out loud in front of everyone? They didn't think of whispering it to Miss Mattie.

"Jessica, go see if she's outside anywhere, and tell her to get in here right now." Miss Mattie's voice sounded a little edgy.

Jessica left the room, not knowing what to do. How was she going to get Matilda back to the room. Outside the room, tears began to roll down her face. She bumped into someone, and looking up, she saw Miss Lillie, her last year's teacher.

"Jessica, honey, whatever is the matter?" Miss Lillie asked.

"Oh, Miss Lillie, I'm in trouble. Matilda's in trouble. I don't know what to do." The words tumbled out of her mouth so fast it was hard to understand her.

"Whoa, slow down, Tell me what's wrong, Jessica."

Jessica started to cry harder. She looked up at Miss Lillie's kind face and choked back her tears. "The elastic on Matilda's bloomers broke and they fell down," she began to explain, "right out on the playground. She's in the outhouse. I have to get her, but how can she come into the schoolhouse with her bloomers down around her feet?"

"She needs a safety pin," Miss Lillie suggested in her calm sweet voice.

"I don't have one," Jessica wailed.

"Now Jessica, don't cry. Wait here and I'll find a safety pin for Matilda." Miss Lillie's voice was so reassuring, that Jessica stopped crying, wiped her eyes, and stood waiting for

Miss Lillie to return. She glanced warily back at her room door. What if Miss Mattie saw her standing there?

Before she could worry too much, Miss Lillie was back and handed her two big safety pins. Matilda wiped her tears with one hand and clutched the pins with the other, as she raced around the corner and on toward the outhouse.

Matilda had given up on getting any help. She could see herself sitting in that old outhouse all evening and in the dark nighttime. Maybe no one would ever find her and she would die there with only her bones left.

When Jessica came in she was sitting in the corner crying. "Why did you leave me, Jessica? What happened to Penny? Why didn't someone help me?"

"I don't know why. I guess Penney was scared. I guess we were all scared to say anything to Miss Mattie. Never mind that—here's two pins. We can pin your bloomers good and tight."

They gathered the top of the bloomers up to the waist and put a pin in each side, pulling the top tight. Matilda dried her tear-stained face on her sleeve and they raced for the schoolhouse.

Miss Mattie eyed Matilda as she sat down in her seat. "Matilda, why are you late?"

Matilda opened her mouth to speak, but the words would not come out.

She saw Miss Mattie begin to write. She knew what she was writing. It was the dreaded note.

"Since you seem to have no reason for being late, you will take this note to your father." This was one of those times when Miss Mattie seemed cool and far away.

Matilda didn't get much from her lessons that afternoon. Her thoughts were on the note and her father's warning, "One more time of deliberately breaking rules, and you are never to mention a pony to me again." Over and over these thoughts raced through her mind.

As they walked home from school, Jessica tried to comfort her. "Why didn't you tell Miss Mattie?"

"I couldn't." was all Matilda could say.

"You can tell your papa."

"No! I can't tell Papa about my bloomers falling off."

"You can tell your mama."

"They said they wouldn't listen to any more excuses."

"I can go home with you and tell them."

"No. I have to go by myself." Matilda did not want any friends around when Papa said the dreaded words.

When she arrived home and went inside, her mother was too busy getting supper to pay much attention to her. She asked the usual questions, "How was school today?" Matilda knew her mother didn't really want to know, because she didn't wait for a reply as she went on to say, "We're having chocolate mousse tonight for dessert, your favorite."

Matilda set her syrup bucket on the shelf and went into the parlor where Papa always sat when he came home. Sometimes Matilda would help Papa take off his shoes and put on the house slippers Mama had given him for Christmas. She laid the teacher's note on Papa's chair and went outside to sit on the steps.

"I don't want to see him when he comes up the walk," she thought, so she got up and went into the back yard. She climbed up into the little Harvest apple tree and sat on the lowest limb with her feet dangling. She sat there a long time and thought of many things, but her thoughts always came back to horses, the beautiful elegant creatures called horses. Finally she heard Papa's voice calling from the back door. Slowly she dropped to the ground and walked to the house.

Papa stepped out onto the back step. He held Miss Mattie's note in his hand. "Young lady, do you have anything to say about this?"

Matilda looked down at her shoes. She shook her head.

"You know what this means?"

Matilda nodded.

"All right. You are never to mention a pony to me again."

Papa closed the door. Matilda stood still where she was. When she heard her mother call "Supper", she slipped into the house and ran up the stairs and into her room. She threw herself down on her bed and buried her face in her pillow. She cried and cried until she could cry no longer. After that, she lay there a long time staring out the window. She heard voices downstairs, then her mother's voice calling her. She went to the head of the stairs and looked down.

"Come down, Matilda," her mother called.

"I don't want to come down, Mama."

"You must come down," Mama said in a kind but stern voice.

Matilda slowly came down the stairs. Mama and Papa were in the parlor. Jessica and her mother were there, too.

Mama came over and put her arm around Matilda. "Honey, Jessica and her mother have told your Papa and me what happened today at school. It was not your fault. I don't understand why you did not tell your teacher, and why you didn't tell us when you came home."

Matilda looked at her father. He was smiling and he nodded to her. "You told me not to make excuses," Matilda reminded him, beginning to feel tears coming into her eyes again.

"Matilda, when you know you're right, you should talk anyway."

Jessica's mother voiced a spirited complaint. "I think it's too bad the girls didn't feel they could tell Miss Mattie. She should have known Matilda had a good reason for being in that old outhouse."

Mama spoke up. "Well, Matilda, thank your friends for coming over and clearing this up for you, and I'll never again say, 'don't talk.'"

Matilda gave Jessica a hug and thanked her mother as they left to go home.

"Now young lady, Mama said, "you come and eat your supper. And how about your favorite dessert, chocolate mousse?"

While she ate, Papa sat down with her and talked about going to Clay Corners on Saturday to see if that Indian pony was still for sale. "I'd like to have seen you on your way to the outhouse with all the girls circled around you," Papa said, laughing.

Mama scolded him. "It wasn't funny, Papa."

"I know it wasn't. Matilda, you had a really bad day today, but when you look back on the day your bloomers fell down, don't you think that someday you can laugh about it?"

Matilda took one spoonful of chocolate mousse, looked at the pleasant smile on Papa's face and smiled, took another spoonful and giggled, then before she knew it, she was laughing. Papa started laughing again and Mama joined in. She was laughing away all the troubles she had experienced that day, trouble with falling bloomers, trouble with Miss Mattie, and trouble with Papa's rules. Then Archie walked in and wanted to know what was so funny.

Papa stopped laughing long enough to say, "Archie, be thankful you do not wear dresses, for if you did, you might lose your underwear someday."

Archie looked puzzled. Mama patted his arm as she told him, "Archie, someday Matilda will explain it to you. Right now, let's all have another helping of chocolate mousse."

So with the taste of chocolate all mixed up with the sound of laughter, and the promise of a Saturday trip to Clay's Corner to buy a pony, a very bad day turned into a very good one—a very good one indeed.

RED ROSES FOR MISS LILLIE

The telephone rang two longs and one short.

"Our number, Josie. Shall I get it?"

"Sure. See who it is, Lillie."

I'd known Josie all my life, so she never called me "Miss" unless she was around school. "It's for you, Josie," I called. "That sounded like Maude Miller trying to change her voice. Why would she be trying to fool me?"

I knew what was going on, but I suppose it was more fun for them to try to keep it secret. I knew the community always had a big dinner the last day of school. And when a teacher left to go to another school, they always gave the teacher a gift. I really wished they wouldn't, but stopping them would be like trying to stop a greased pig and would hurt their feelings and spoil all their fun.

It was hard to believe the school year was almost over, and that evening I sat there on the back porch at Josie's house, thinking about the three years at Springdale School. I thought of the good people of the community I had grown to love and respect. It would be hard to say good-bye, especially to the children.

The two-room school had forty-three students from first through eighth grades. Mr. Rutherford taught the upper grades, and although he wasn't leaving, he, too, would get gifts. I had a whole shoe-box full of handkerchiefs I had received in the past—handkerchiefs of fine cotton lisle, linen, and silk, with lace, crocheting, or tatting around the edges.

It was with a feeling of sadness that we had finished cleaning out cupboards and desks, and had sent home all the lost mittens, and hats, and scarves. The eighth graders had enjoyed a graduation night. They each got to make a speech since there were only four of them. I would miss the older students, too, since I had taught some of them the previous years, and had helped in all the programs.

Then there was Josie. How could I leave Josie? I'd never find another one to stay with who'd be like Josie. She made me feel so at home, and she made life so much fun. Her husband, Reuben was the practical one, taking everything in a serious vein.

It was Reuben now who jolted me out of my melancholy thoughts. "Need any shoes half-soled?" he asked.

"Yes, to tell you the truth, I do. But I think the uppers are worn out, too. It would be like putting new wine in old bottles. Besides, my papa would feel hurt if I didn't let him do it."

"If you say so," Reuben answered agreeably, putting an old shoe over the shoe last.

Interspersed with Reuben's hammering, the neighbor's voices came across the road to us. Reuben had rented the little house back of his house to Cleopatra and her two boys, Jackson, eleven, and Jefferson who was six. Cleopatra had told us that she named them after presidents, and that she had no idea where her mother got her name. Jefferson, the boy in my room, was a good boy, but Jackson was a trial to everyone.

When Reuben let up on the hammering, I recognized the husky, heavy voice of Jackson.

"Why does Jefferson always get the goodest of everything? He gets the biggest piece of pie; he finds the reddest apples; and he gets the goodest teacher. Why do he always get the goodest?"

"Why do he always get the goodest? Could be 'cause he takes what he gets and makes the goodest out of it."

"Anyway, I wish Iz in Miss Lillie's room."

"You'd have to behave, boy, just like you do in Mr. Rutherford's room."

Jefferson's voice was not so easy to make out, but I thought he was saying, "Mama, when will the roses bloom?"

"Jefferson, you asked me that ten thousand times. I tell you they'll bloom in time."

86

"School's almost out, Mama. I need the roses to give Miss Lillie."

"I'm not givin' no roses to Mr. Rutherford."

Then came a final remark form Cleopatra. "Them roses are showin' buds now. They gonna bloom in time."

"Poor Jefferson. If the roses don't bloom in time, I'll have to come back to Josie's to get them," I thought.

As their voices faded out, I heard Reuben talking to himself. "There now, I've got me a new pair of shoes." He took the shoe off the last and brought it over for me to inspect.

"Heh!" he said, in a tone unusually cheerful for him, "did you know the Sharps are coming down this evening? We've got to play one more game of 'Hide the Thimble' before you leave." One thing Reuben did enjoy was an evening of visiting and games with the Sharps.

Josie washed a big bowl of Winesaps and Jonathons and made a double batch of ginger cookies. They would be gone when the evening was over.

The Sharps lived only a mile away and they walked in about dark. As John Sharp came in, he called out, "Ever hear the story of the empty box, Reuben?" Reuben always bit; I think he enjoyed biting on John's jokes.

"No, what about it," Reuben asked.

"Nothing in it," John answered, guffawing, delighted that Reuben had bit. You could laugh with John Sharp even when nothing was funny. He was round as a barrel and he shook all over when he laughed.

We were in the middle of our second game of "Hide the Thimble," when Jefferson Wills stuck his nose against the screen door and asked, "Did you saw her? Did you saw my cat?"

"No, Jefferson, we didn't see your cat."

Jackson's face appeared right behind him. "Jefferson," he scolded, "you just smelled Josie's cookies. Mama's gonna strap you."

"Not so," Jefferson whimpered, ready to cry. "My cat is gone."

"She's under the bed, I tell you."

Josie filled a sack with cookies and took it to the door with three apples. "Give one to your mama," she said.

"And Jefferson," I called out, "look under the bed when you get home."

"All right, Miss Lillie, I will." He still had his nose pressed to the screen. "Miss Lillie, " he asked, "do you like roses—red roses?"

"I surely do, Jefferson. I like red roses better than most anything." That seemed to satisfy Jefferson, and his little face faded into the night. We finished the last "I Spy" in "Hide the Thimble," and started a game of Pinochle. Sharp's youngest boy Seth stood by my knee.

"Miss Lillie, " he said, "you gonna get two quilts. I saw one at the church. Two quilts and a..."

"Sh," his mother hushed him.

"Oh, well, now that she knows, we might as well tell her, " John Sharp said, laughing it off. "Miss Lillie, you might as well know the Methodist ladies are making you a quilt; and the Baptist ladies couldn't be out-done, so they're making one, too."

"John Sharp, you're worse than a kid. Can't you keep your mouth shut," his wife scolded. John responded with his usual big laugh.

The last day at school finally came. I went early to finish the report I had to turn in at the county superintendent's office. We had cleaned desks the day before and had taken everything home. The room looked sadly empty with the pictures and charts all down off the walls.

By nine o'clock, the wagons were beginning to pull into the school-yard. Thatcher Brown had driven his big mules.

"They must be at least sixteen hands high," I heard one of the men remark outside my window.

"Seventeen, Thatcher claims," his neighbor responded. "I think Thatcher brings 'em just to show 'em off."

Now I could hear a bang, bang, banging, as the men moved the desks in the room next to mine. They were setting up the long food table in there.

"All the food will be kept covered until noon," Josie told

me, "and they have a wooden chest of ice for the food that needs to be kept cold."

I saw a half dozen women armed with fly swatters, and sticky fly paper was lying on top of the old organ and on the piano. Curls of sticky paper hung from the gas lights.

By eleven, it seemed that everyone in the whole community was there. And the food—what a sight. The table was the full length of the room, and was covered with dishes. The merchants in town had donated soda pop and there was enough for an army. The bottles floated in a tub of ice water, and cases of pop were stacked ready to replace what was taken out.

Ball games and horse-shoe games were in progress. One of the Jones boys had ridden their donkey, and an occasional long bray added to the noise. It almost stopped the games when the Crandles drove into the school-yard in their new Buick touring car.

The big girls were hanging around with nothing to do, so I suggested they help me carry my records and a sack of belongings to Josie's house, as it was only a quarter mile down the road. When we got to Josie's house, the girls stayed outside, playing with the collie, while I took the sack inside. I was walking out when I heard the phone ring. "Five Shorts. I think that's Cleopatra's mother's ring—Why aren't they at school?" I decided to listen in, as I thought someone might be sick. Carefully, I took down the receiver.

It was Cleopatra shouting into the telephone. "No, he's sittin' here bawlin' his eyes out. Says he's not goin' to school. You know for three months, every day, he's asked me, 'When's the roses goin' to bloom, Mama?' so he could take some to Miss Lillie. Yesterday they bloomed out so pretty, and he was really happy. You never saw a boy so happy. Then last night in the middle of the night, a herd of wild cattle came runnin' through the yard and trampled those bushes into the dirt, right into the ground. I hope they got some scratches. They missed my garden. I'd almost rather they'd took the garden than the roses. I don't know what to do—I hate to see my boy grievin' so."

Now Cleopatra's mother's voice. "Now you listen to me,

Cleopatra. Behind my house, in a little draw, is a clump of rose bushes. Guess no one knew they's there, 'cause they're still there. I know they are, because I'm lookin' at them right

now. Tell that boy to get down here and get these roses."

Carefully, I hung up the receiver, gathered up the girls, and hurried back to the celebration. Poor Jefferson. In the rush of things, I hadn't noticed he wasn't at school.

At noon, the chairman of the board rang the bell and everyone gathered at the door. He made a few remarks about a good school year, then asked me to come up onto the porch. He made a little speech about how they all appreciated me and I felt like crying. They presented the two quilts little Seth had told me about and a cedar chest the men had hired Hans Jenersen to make. Everyone clapped and cheered after I thanked them and told them how much I'd miss them. I cut my remarks short when I heard someone sniffle. Besides, I knew everyone was getting hungry.

As I stepped down off the porch, there was Jefferson with his bunch of red roses, smiling through a tear-streaked face. I sat down on the porch and pulled him down beside me.

I whispered to him, "Jefferson, this is the best gift of all. RED ROSES—my favorite. Thank you, Jefferson for my beautiful red roses." And I think Jefferson was finally feeling supremely happy on that last day of school.

MOSTLY SIMON

I had left my little one-room schoolhouse behind and had come to Big Town. A veteran teacher gave me an assessment of my roomful of children. "They just seem to gravitate toward crises, sometimes even creating them," she said.

"Oh dear," I thought. "Why do I get a group like this my first year in town?"

To cheer me she added, "They are very bright children, though and good-hearted."

Into October, I thought back on her assessment and found it to have been very accurate. It was on a Friday at noon recess, that I finished an apple after checking spelling papers, and wandered over to a west window. A movement on the north playground caught my eye. A small loose-knit group of children were moving toward the south door, dragging something along and gathering followers as they went.

"Oh, oh, they're mine," I observed. "I might have known." I knew who would be in the middle of it, too. Who was always in the middle of everything? Simon—Mostly Simon—as he was beginning to be called.

"Oh, horrors, they are dragging a child! Why didn't they go to the playground teacher?" I said aloud, as I rushed out of the room and down to the south hall.

I met them just as they came through the door. Simon, in the center of the group of children, huffed and puffed as he dragged Teddy Berens through the doorway. He was gripping one of Teddy's arms and Roseanne had the other. Simon's usually ruddy cheeks were redder than ever, looking like two McIntosh apples. His chestnut curls were matted to his

forehead from perspiration, and his brown eyes sparkled like river water in the morning sunlight. His smile was triumphant; he had accomplished his mission.

The shouting was intense, with each small voice eager to be top reporter. Then, like popcorn flying out of a lidless popper, a pronouncement would come screaming through: "Teddy's got lice."

And there was Teddy in the midst of it all, a smile on his cotton-topped face, as he basked in the spotlight of rare attention. I reached down and took his hand, rescuing him from the grips of Simon and Roseanne. Although he seemed imperturbed by his rough treatment, I was not. He was sparsely built for seven years and looked a mite fragile.

I held up my hand for silence and motioned for the children to follow me. Back in room 107, they crept into their seats and stared at me as I wrote at my desk.

"Teddy, take this note to the nurse," I directed.

"I'll go with him," Simon offered.

"I'll go, Miss Lillie," Roseanne challenged.

"He knows the way; he had a skinned knee yesterday," I countered.

"Now," I looked around the room. "Does anyone want to talk about this?"

Silence enveloped the room.

"Did you handle it right?" I prodded.

Simon was quick to respond to this. "Oh yes, Miss Lillie. If you got lice, you gotta go home. We had to bring him in."

"Did you do it right?" I pursued.

Kelly Baker spoke up. "Miss Lillie, maybe he was embarrassed."

"We shouldna drug him," Jimmy Snow suggested.

"Whose idea was it?" I asked.

No one spoke.

"Anne?" I knew I could always depend on Anne for the truth.

"Well, Miss Lillie, we all did it. We all helped."

"But who suggested dragging Teddy into the schoolhouse like that?"

Anne's voice came softly through the silence. "I'm not

sure, Miss Lillie, but I think it was mostly Simon."

"Mostly Simon." How many times had I heard that little phrase?

Teddy was at my elbow now with a note from the nurse. "No sign of lice," Nurse Brown had written.

"So—you don't have lice, Teddy. Why did you say you did?"

"My Mom said I did." Teddy twisted first on one foot, then on the other, both hands in his pockets and a sheepish grin on his face.

"Your mother said you had head lice?"

"Yeah. This morning, I said, 'Mom, my head itches,' and Mom said, 'Oh lord no, not head lice!'"

I turned to the room. "Well children, Teddy doesn't have head lice. I hope you think twice before you take things into your hands the next time, especially you, Simon."

As the days came and went, Young Simon found a solid place in my mind and heart. His work was always done on time and without error, yet he always found time to be aware of everything going on around him. If anything fell to the floor, it was Simon who picked it up; he was at the door to open it for anyone coming or going; he mopped up spills, found lost articles, and would have run all the errands, had I not divided them among the children.

One morning in October there was talk about some jerseys having been stolen from the high school football field that bordered the elementary playground. "Well, this is one problem I don't have to worry about," I thought as I walked down to my room.

Miss Donovan, the principal, met me in the hall. "You heard about the stolen jerseys?" she asked.

"Yes, oh yes, I heard about that."

"Well, guess who took them?"

I hesitated. Then I gasped. "Not Simon?"

"Yes, Simon," and she started laughing. She stopped laughing when she saw the look on my face.

"That child!" I exploded, wondering how she could stand there with a smile on her face. "Now wait a minute," I said. "Miss Donovan, Simon is always getting into trouble, but he's no thief. He's not a bad child. He just takes things into his own hands—things beyond his maturity to handle. Then he gets into trouble."

"I know, my dear," Miss Donovan spoke softly to soothe my ruffled feelings, "Wait until you hear the whole story. Thank goodness, it's been thoroughly covered, so I don't think we'll have to do much about it. Here's the story. Simon, Roseanne, and Teddy were walking home when they spotted the jerseys. They were so dirty, according to Simon, that they decided to take them home and wash them. They started to sneak them into Simon's house, but Simon's mother was doing the laundry. They were going to Roseanne's house, but Roseanne had told the boys that her mother had eyes in the back of her head, and could see everything. They ended up at Teddy's house, because Teddy's Mom never sees anything, and if she does, she doesn't care.

They got the jerseys washed and hung them out to dry. Simon and Roseanne went home then, for by that time, they could hear their mothers beating the bushes for them."

"Simon and his bad judgement," I lamented.

Miss Donovan continued. "They did do one thing they knew to be wrong. Simon and Roseanne told their mothers that the reason they were late getting home was that they had gone home with Teddy to help him carry his homework, as you had given him so much to do, he couldn't carry it all himself." Miss Donovan doubled over laughing. It was beginning to look funny to me, too.

"Mr. Wyland said they came marching in this morning and laid the spanking clean jerseys on the desk."

"How they ever found his office in that building, I'll never know," Miss Donovan commented.

"Oh, Simon and Roseanne could find their way through the galaxy," I reminded her.

As I started to leave, she said, "Mr. Wyland thinks Simon is some boy. He said Simon did most of the talking. He was the one who engineered it all. Yes, according to Mr. Wyland, it was mostly Simon."

"Mostly Simon," I echoed, as I went to my room.

I scheduled a trip to the art museum for the first of April. The night before the trip, a light snow fell, and a wind blew in out of the northwest. At twelve-thirty, we were bundled up, excited, and ready to go. The walk to the museum was a short one, but by the time we came in sight of the museum, snow was whirling around, and it had turned bitter cold. As we waited on the corner for the street car to pass, I noticed a young mother with a child in her arms and a toddler hanging onto her coat. I smiled in sympathy at her plight in the turbulent weather.

"We just came in on the train," she explained. "We're going up to my husband's office and we'll ride home with him. We live on the other side of town and he has a closed carriage."

The last child crossed the street and started south toward the museum steps. They had to pass an alley, and I noticed a Model T making a turn to take the alley. I made sure all the children were safely across the alley, then I turned, and I saw the toddler break away from his mother and run back into the street. I saw in an instant why he had done so. A vagrant balloon was being whipped about by the wind, and as it blew in front of the ford, the child followed. At the same time, a wagon pulled by a team of large gray mules came out of the alley. There were yells and screams and a screech of brakes and tires.

I heard Simon yell, "The baby!" and saw him jump in front of the car. The next thing I saw was Simon pushing the baby out of the path of the moving car.

"My baby!" the mother screamed.

A room mother was at my elbow. "Take the children on into the building," I shouted above the howling wind and the shouts of people. I rushed into the street, afraid of what I would see. Coming around the corner, I saw him lying there— our Simon. A passerby was now holding the toddler, who was whimpering, "Wanta balloon."

I dropped to my knees beside Simon. His face was so white. "This can't be Simon, our Simon," I thought, "our Simon with the ruddy cheeks, the cherry-red lips, the sparkling eyes. Oh, God, don't let him be hurt bad."

One leg seemed to be twisted out of shape. A hysterical man was saying, "When I turned, I didn't see the children." The mother with the toddler was tugging at my sleeve. "The boy's name?" she asked. "I must know how he does. He saved my boy's life."

"It's Jefferson School," I answered numbly. "Call them."

Then Simon was on a stretcher, being carried away. Inside I found a phone and called the school. When someone finally answered, I rushed my message. "Tell Miss Donovan I'm at the museum. Tell her I need her. Send some mothers to help with the children. Get someone to go to Simon's house and tell his mother he's been hurt, and we don't know how badly. You'd better have someone take her to the hospital."

Miss Donovan was only minutes away, but it seemed hours before she got there. I climbed in and sat on the edge of the seat as we drove toward the hospital. She had taken the side curtains off, and the wind whipped through the car, chilling us to the bone. As we ran up the steps of the hospital building, I was shaking all over from the tension and the chilly ride. We found the room where he was being examined and waited outside the room, pacing back and forth.

Simon's mother came running in. "Where is he?" she cried out.

We pointed to the door and she pushed through. Miss Donovan and I went to the door and listened. We slipped through the door and saw a doctor and a nurse hovering over the bed. The doctor stepped back and Simon's mother clutched his arm.

"Doctor, I'm his mother," she pleaded.

The doctor put his arm around her. "We are lucky," he said. "Preliminary exams show only a slight concussion. The worst thing is a badly busted leg, but nothing we can't fix. As I said, we're lucky—he's lucky, a lucky boy."

"Thank God," Simon's mother said softly.

Back at school, the children were milling around the room. "We couldn't settle them down," a mother said. I was glad to hear the dismissal bell, signalling the end of the day.

We got the children into their seats and explained to them that Simon would miss some school, but that he was going to be all right.

As the last one left, a reporter from the city paper stepped in. "Say, that was something. We want to run a story on it tomorrow. Tell me what you know about the little hero who saved the baby."

"Tell you about Simon?—Mostly Simon?" I smiled as I stared at the empty seat, forth row back. "Sit down," I suggested. "It will take a while to do that."

OF ALL THE MEMORIES OF THE PAST, SCHOOL MEMORIES ARE THE ONES THAT LAST.